Tribal Fires

Judy Moresi

L & L Dreamspell
London, Texas

Cover and Interior Design by L & L Dreamspell

Copyright © 2011 Judy Moresi. All rights reserved. No part of this publication may be reproduced, stored in a retrieval system or transmitted in any form or by any means, electronic, mechanical, photocopying, recording or otherwise without the prior written permission of the copyright holder, except for brief quotations used in a review.

This is a work of fiction, and is produced from the author's imagination. People, places and things mentioned in this novel are used in a fictional manner.

ISBN: 978-1-60318-419-9

Library of Congress Control Number: 2011931749

Visit us on the web at www.lldreamspell.com

Published by L & L Dreamspell
Printed in the United States of America

ACKNOWLEDGMENTS

To research Tribal Fires, I attended many powwows in St. Louis and St. Charles County, Missouri, and met a lot of wonderful people. A powwow is both a social and a religious event. Native Americans from across the United States and Canada gather to celebrate weddings and births, share the sorrow of a death among them, to pray for healing and take up a collection for those in need, and to commemorate and welcome home the return of their young warriors from the Gulf War, Afghanistan, and Iraq. They are a proud, kind people. Taking me under their wing, they wrapped a colorful shawl around my waist to cover my jeans and gave me a feather fan to carry, walked on each side of me as an escort, and taught me how to dance in the Sacred Circle. They explained the titles of the other dancers, the direction I must go, and how to avoid the men who danced in a trancelike frenzy. I asked and received their permission to take pictures, then brought them copies when I revisited. I learned that when they receive a gift, they must reciprocate and I was given a lovely feather and bead necklace and their friendship. They chose an Indian name for me that translates "Woman With Heart of Indian." Truly, I shall carry them forever in my heart.

I want to thank the gang at Coffee & Critique for their suggestions, for sharing their talent, and for their all-around rowdiness. A round of applause to the wonderful staff at L&L Dreamspell: Lisa Smith, Linda Houle, and my editor, Cindy Davis. Thank you to Dr. Mary Case, our greater St. Louis and surrounding communities' Medical Examiner, for her expert advice. And a big "thank you" to all the people who bought my first mystery novel, Widow's Walk, and to the people who helped me get it into the hands of those readers: booksellers, librarians, book reviewers, radio interviewer, and book clubs and conference organizers who asked me to speak about the wonderful, magical world of writing.

I especially want to convey my love and appreciation to my family for their moral support and never losing faith in my work: Tom I, Tom II, Scott, Rachele, Veronica, Tom III, and Sylvia Rose. A special thanks to my husband Tom and good friend Maggie Sapanara Wise who have faithfully helped me at book signings and conferences. You guys rock!

And above all I want to thank my grandfather, Silas Corbit Chandler, who had enough Cherokee blood in him to claim free land, who taught me how to sit silently in the woods and draw wild animals to us, and although I never knew her, to my great-grandmother, Susan Pitman Carwile, for the Fox blood she passed down to me. I am the sum of all those who went before me and follow after.

Any inaccuracies or misinterpretations in this work of fiction were unintentional.

Dedication

To my greatest accomplishments, my sons Thomas Robert Moresi II and Scott Nicholas Moresi—two fine, upstanding, and handsome men of whom I am so proud.

One

Shea McKenna's pulse quickened as she centered thin cross hairs on the base of a buffalo horn. Sweat trickled across her forehead, but experience steadied her hand. This would be her best shot of the day.

"It's a forgery!" Ethan Brumley's voice boomed across the museum storeroom.

Shea jerked away from the Nikon's viewfinder, her thumb poised on its shutter release. "What? A forgery?"

The old registrar, his back twisted like a corkscrew by scoliosis, sat hunched over a cluttered worktable. He peered through an illuminated magnifying glass attached to headgear perched on his bald pate. Knobby hands, clothed in white work gloves to protect the relics, shook as he slowly rotated a Sioux war lance.

"Miss McKenna, you need to come see this if you're going to understand how to spot counterfeits."

"That's your bag. I just take pictures," she called over her shoulder and returned to her camera's viewfinder. "In three days, I'm outta here. Mexico, baby. *Hasta la vista.*"

She'd landed an assignment on the Yucatan Peninsula for *Ancient Cultures* magazine. Someone had discovered a Mayan temple at the Guatemalan border.

"Suit yourself."

Ethan was right though. She needed to see what forged artifacts looked like if she were to recognize them at a dig site. Shea had majored in Archeology at the University of Missouri, but that was eight years ago. Her knowledge of Native American artifacts came nowhere near Ethan's.

She wove her way through a maze of crates and boxes to where he sat on a metal stool. Brushing a wisp of long auburn hair from her eyes, she peeked over his shoulder. The pungent aroma of Ben Gay tweaked her nose.

He looked up, indignation etched on his age-puckered face. "This Sioux war lance, Miss McKenna, is a copy."

As he slowly turned the weapon, glare from the overhead lights glinted along its wooden shaft. Bone beads dangling on leather strips clacked a hollow rattle. A dried splash of red at the base of the flint spearhead reminded Shea of blood.

"It looks authentic," she said. "Wouldn't the restorer have noticed?"

The old man peered over the top of his horn-rimmed glasses. "Young lady, I've been an artifact registrar since the Nixon administration. I know counterfeit when I see it."

She bent closer. "How can you tell?"

He gifted her with a condescending smile. "To an untrained eye, a fake would be hard to spot. A forger simply cannibalizes damaged artifacts that are beyond repair to make a new lance."

"Isn't that what a restorer does?"

Ethan's voice raised an octave. "A reputable restorer *does not* create a new piece that hasn't existed before and pass it off as the real item. *Never.*"

"And that's what you suspect."

He ran a white-gloved hand along the lance's smooth shaft. "The American Indian was an excellent hunter, capable of piercing a buffalo's hide or driving a stone blade completely through a man."

She squinted at the crusty red stain at the base of the spearhead. "What happens if it isn't genuine?"

"If it came to the museum as such, our experts would be quite embarrassed and their credibility damaged. Knowledge and reputation are all a historian has to offer."

"Who verified it?"

"Let me see...that would be Native American expert Tom Bennett from the Santa Fe museum and Cullen Gerard, director and acquisitions officer for the Gateway to the West Historical Society." A pensive frown crossed the old historian's face. "Oh, and Cheek Larson, an artifact dealer." The corners of his mouth drooped in distaste. "Mr. Larson has a knack for ferreting out relics from private collections and shabby roadside museums. He's part Indian...and crafty."

She'd heard of Gerard and Bennett, but not the third man. "What did you mean by 'if the lance *came* to the museum as a forgery'?"

"It's possible someone switched it after the authentication." He arched a thinning brow. "That wouldn't look good for Miss Scott."

Ann Scott was her friend and the Missouri Westward Museum's first woman curator. Surely Ethan didn't think her guilty of fraud? She confided to Shea she hoped to be curator of a New York museum someday. Or, dare she dream, the Smithsonian.

"Ann? Dealing in forgeries? No way," Shea said.

"Whatever happens in this museum reflects on Miss Scott. If she used bad judgment, her credibility's tarnished." He threw his gloves on the table. "Her career in antiquities will be over. Remember what happened with Piltdown Man?"

She remembered reading about the anthropological scam. A man's cranium attached to the jawbone of an ape.

"Then there's the Shroud of Turin, a controversial piece of cloth batted back and forth for centuries concerning its authenticity. And the Hitler diaries." Ethan clicked his tongue in derision. "You can see how one little slip can destroy a reputation."

"How valuable is the original lance?"

"Restored, in the neighborhood of twenty thousand dollars."

Shea whistled. "Nice neighborhood."

He scanned the worktable. She followed his gaze as he zeroed in on an Arikara bone knife, a cluster of Navajo pottery, and a hand-carved wooden bowl of the Woodlands Indian era amidst a jumble of catalog sheets.

"A tidy fortune can be made dealing in forged artifacts," he said. "Millions of dollars, if undetected."

And greed could turn a friend into a stranger.

Still, Shea couldn't imagine Ann with her manicured nails and Prada suit skulking around late at night switching artifacts.

Ethan must've seen disbelief in her eyes. "Mind you, I'm not accusing Miss Scott. She's a delightful young woman and her curatorship has been without blemish."

Shea persisted, "I can't believe the restorer wouldn't have noticed—"

Ethan's hand shot out and clutched her arm. Thin arthritic fingers dug into her wrist as he stared wide-eyed at something behind her.

Unnerved, Shea whipped around, then gasped in awe at the majestic Indian filling the storeroom doorway.

Two

Hair shiny as a raven's wing fell across the handsome Indian's broad shoulders. At his temple, a red feather attached to a leather strip secured his braided forelock. Shea's gaze traveled along the tight cut of his black jeans, down muscular thighs, to feet she expected to see shod in moccasins. She was surprised to find black tasseled Gucci loafers. When her attention strayed back to his bronze-colored face, she saw he was smiling at her.

"Hello." His voice sounded like wind whispering through a deep canyon.

A pleasant shiver tripped along her spine. The walls of the museum fell away, and they stood atop a mountain. Overhead, a lone eagle soared across an azure sky.

"Miss McKenna," the eagle squawked.

No, it was Ethan.

"This is Blade Santee. Future chief of the Dakota Sioux. *And the artisan who restored this lance.*"

The warning tone in Ethan's voice dampened her enthusiasm. He seemed concerned Blade overheard them discussing the possible fraud.

She refused to jump to conclusions. The old registrar already suspected Ann, Cullen Gerard, Tom Bennett, and some schmuck named Cheek Larson of collusion. Now he seemed determined to add to his list the most magnificent example of the Native American gene pool she'd ever seen.

"Hello. My name is Shea McKenna." She returned Blade's smile.

"Hello, Shea."

The earth stood still. Planets ceased to orbit. Stars collided, and the sun crashed into the ocean.

She sighed. These flights of fantasy every time Blade spoke would have to stop. Her last meaningful relationship had ended over a year ago due to her busy travel schedule. Or was it because she couldn't find a man who didn't try to limit her? Whichever, she recognized her reaction for what it was. A hormone rush.

Nothing to take seriously.

She tugged at the neck of her T-shirt, letting in air to cool her body—and thoughts.

"You work for the museum?" Blade asked, his dark eyes searching hers.

"Yes. I mean, no. I mean..."

Oh, for heaven's sake! This was ridiculous. She'd witnessed a sunrise from the top of Cheops' great pyramid at Giza on a clear Egyptian morning. Visited Inca ruins in the lush green mountains of Peru. Floated a rickety junket on the unbelievably blue China Sea. She'd enjoyed all of this with deliberate composure.

Why would one good-looking Indian take her breath away?

His smile widened.

That's why.

Embarrassed that she was acting like a smitten school girl, Shea squared her shoulders. "I'm a freelance photographer."

Ethan coughed his obvious disapproval at her behavior.

Blade's gaze tracked to the old man and the lance. He moved closer, towering over him. "Are you ready for my men to bring over more artifacts?"

"Y-yes," Ethan stuttered.

Shea watched him wilt under Blade's penetrating eyes.

Straightening his crooked spine as best he could, the old man regained his composure. "I haven't quite finished with this lance, however. It would not do for me to let a fake slip by."

Unbelievable. He was baiting Blade. She admired the old man's courage, but she didn't see any reason to antagonize the

Indian until the lance had been verified. Especially if Blade was innocent. Even more so if he proved guilty. Otherwise, they might never recover the real lance or learn how extensive the swindle.

"Everything so far has proven authentic," she interceded. "You do beautiful work."

"Thank you." His eyes never strayed from Ethan or the lance. Abruptly, he stalked out.

Ethan's scrawny body relaxed.

So the old historian wasn't as brave as he acted.

Or maybe not so thoroughly convinced.

She patted his shoulder. "I'm sure we'll find the lance authentic."

For Ann's sake, Shea hoped so. And for Blade's. She hated to think the gorgeous hunk might be corrupt. What a waste that would be. And she hated the thought of working under the strained conditions the accusation would bring.

Ethan slid off the stool, determination fixed in his milky eyes. "I must show the lance to Miss Scott," he mumbled as he scuttled out the storeroom door, the war lance clutched in his hand.

Three

"Wait a minute, I'll come with you." Shea followed Ethan to the offices on the museum's second floor. As much as she disliked confrontations, she hated not knowing what was going on even more. Ann's career wouldn't be the only one to suffer if they were mixed up in a fraud.

They found her in a meeting room sorting through a batch of yellowed papers at a mahogany conference table. Matching shelves piled with more stacks of paper lined the wall to the right. On the opposite side of the room, multi-paned windows reached from floor to ceiling. The curator spoke into a phone cradled between her shoulder and ear.

"We received some last minute RSVPs, Mr. Raguzzi. Fifty more people." Ann paused, raking back her blonde pageboy. "Can't you just throw more stuffed mushrooms on a tray?"

The faster she talked, the faster she sorted the faded papers. Dust particles danced in the morning sunlight around her pink-suited, five-foot-nine-inch frame.

"Phew, these catalog sheets must have been in the vault since the museum opened," she said, then quickly added into the receiver, "No, Mr. Raguzzi, I'm not talking to you. Listen, I can't keep contributing patrons away because the domestic mushroom crop was poor this year. Yes, Mr. Raguzzi, I am now talking to you."

Ann glanced up, noticed Shea and Ethan, and rolled her large green eyes. "Marinated artichoke hearts will be fine." She hung up the phone and sighed. "Caterers."

"Where's your office help?" Shea asked.

"Meg's positioning potted plants in the vestibule for the Patrons Ball tomorrow night. Lena's at Kinko's making sure everything's ready when the photos arrive. They're spiral binding them this year so we can give most of the donations to Blade's people for a clinic."

Ann shot a stricken look at Shea. "The photos will be done in time for the Ball, won't they? Things are okay in the storeroom, aren't they?"

Ethan cut in. "Things are *not* okay in the storeroom."

"What's wrong?" Ann's focus darted from Shea to Ethan to the war lance in his hand.

He laid the artifact on the conference table, its bone beads knocking against the wooden surface. "This lance is a forgery."

Ann's fuchsia lips parted in protest. Before she could speak, a haughty voice intervened.

"Impossible."

Shea turned to see a tall, elegant man dressed in a navy pinstriped suit stride through the doorway. Gray streaked his red hair at the temples, but not a wrinkle creased his face. The scent of expensive cologne followed him into the room, warring with Ethan's Ben Gay ointment.

"Experts authenticated that lance," the newcomer added in the same arrogant tone.

"Then, Mr. Gerard, you'd better find new experts," Ethan shot back.

"Cullen." Ann exhaled his name.

So this was Cullen Gerard, acquisitions officer for the Gateway to the West Historical Society. Shea couldn't help noticing how his mere presence seemed to captivate Ann.

Ethan's retort brought a wry smile to Cullen's patrician features. "Why, Mr. Brumley, I thought you retired."

"Barbara's sick," Ann answered. "I didn't want to call in a registrar we'd never worked with before. I-I thought rehiring Ethan until Barbara recovered would speed things up."

Hands on hips, Ethan returned Cullen's icy stare. "If John Franklin was alive, I'd still be chief registrar for this museum."

"If John Franklin was alive and running the museum like he had been, *everyone* here would be out of a job," Cullen said.

Ethan flushed.

"Franklin's directorship was without distinction," Cullen continued. He seemed to take pleasure in demeaning a dead man. "Fortunately, the board had the foresight to hire me when he died." He nodded at Ann. "To bolster the museum's finances."

"The fact remains," Ethan fumed. "This lance is a forgery."

Afraid the already volatile situation would escalate from bad to abysmal, Shea stepped forward. "Ethan thinks it could've been switched after it was authenticated."

"Afterward? That's not possible." Cullen paused, taking note of Shea for the first time. "And who might you be?"

"Oh, Cullen, I'm sorry." Ann hurried around the conference table. "This is Shea McKenna, the photographer I hired for the catalog and patron's books."

"Well, Miss McKenna, I'm eager to see your work."

"Most of the photos, except for what's in my camera, are being developed as we speak."

"Good. But to dispel your concerns, once artifacts are verified and cataloged, they're transported under armed guard to the restorer's workshop, then returned to the museum storeroom, again under armed guard, rechecked in the catalog, and photographed. A forgery? I can't see how."

Before Shea could respond, Ann edged closer to Cullen, her voice softening. "I didn't expect to see you this morning."

"I'm meeting Cheek Larson here. He's offered to fly me to Santa Fe to look at some Anasazi pottery." His gaze flitted to the doorway. "Here he is now."

A tall, bull of a man with fleshy jowls lumbered into the room. Dark scraggly hair skimmed the collar of a loose-fitting western jacket trimmed with fringe that jiggled as he walked. His brown, pock-marked face and hands had an orange cast.

Cullen motioned to the man. "I believe everyone except Miss McKenna knows him."

Cheek removed his sunglasses. A bracelet made from a rattlesnake's tail circled his thick wrist. He greeted her in a deep monotone. "*Hau kola*."

Shea nodded. Remembering Ethan's professional contempt for the dealer, she decided not to offer her hand. Something about his small piggish eyes and dark scowl made her think he might not give it back.

Cullen carefully handed him the lance. "Brumley thinks this is a forgery. I suggest we have it re-examined by an expert outside the museum."

Shea's sentiments exactly.

"In fact," he added, "I'd be happy to take it with me to Santa Fe and have the Museum of Antiquities verify it."

Ethan lunged for the lance. "It shouldn't leave the museum until its authenticity is settled."

Cheek's grip on the relic tightened. "I vouched for this lance. Me, Cullen, and Tom Bennett. Are you calling us liars, Brumley?"

Ethan shot a look of alarm at Ann. "Miss Scott?"

As if seeking approval, Ann glanced at Cullen before she spoke. "Maybe Ethan's right." She turned to Cheek. "We really shouldn't be touching the lance—or any relic—without wearing gloves. The oils on our skin...we wouldn't want to damage it."

Shea, too, was surprised the men handled the lance so roughly. If it came to a tug of war between Cheek and Ethan, the old man would lose. Of course, if Ethan believed it to be a fake, and Cheek *knew* it to be...

She wiped her hands on her jeans and took hold of the lance above their fists. "I know I don't have a vote in this, but I agree with Ethan. The lance should stay here until it's re-examined." After all, she had her own professional future to think of. She didn't need her name linked to an artifact con, especially if it caused a delay in her schedule. She would be leaving for Mexico in a few days.

Looking like members of a little league baseball team gripping the bat to choose sides, they clung to the lance.

"Cullen, I think they're right," Ann said.

For a moment, he didn't speak, then demurred. "Of course. Just trying to be helpful. And I apologize, Cheek, for Brumley's insensitivity. I'm sure a reasonable explanation will be found."

Briefly, Shea glimpsed the Cullen Gerard who could charm money out of a patron's pocketbook.

Cheek's scowl darkened, but he released the lance.

Cullen turned to Ann. "Have anyone you choose examine it. I insist the Historical Society pay for a new verification. I'm sure we can straighten this out to everyone's satisfaction."

Ann smiled. "Thank you. I—the museum—appreciates all the Society has contributed."

Shea noted Ann's body language, how she leaned toward Cullen, her head cocked to one side. What was going on between her friend and the director?

A movement in the hallway drew their attention. The handsome Indian Shea had met in the storeroom sauntered in.

"Ah, Blade's here," Cullen said. "I'm sure he can clear this up."

Blade Santee's eyes searched the room until they met Shea's. He smiled. Her knees weakened. Cullen was still talking, but all she could hear were doves cooing in the eaves. Embarrassed, she nodded, then glanced away.

Blade's attention switched to the lance, once again in Ethan's possession. "Is there a problem?"

"This man thinks the lance is a fake," Cheek said, sarcasm lacing his words.

"Then this man is mistaken."

Cullen concurred. "Just as I thought. And we'll settle the matter after the Patrons Ball tomorrow night."

"Oh, no." Ann's hand flew to her throat. "The Ball."

"Exactly. We can't have a hint of fraud. The money coming in for the gallery and the clinic would dry up overnight."

So that's why Cullen's so concerned.

"Monday will be soon enough to verify the lance," he assured them. "In the meantime, I suggest we all get back to work." The director glared at Ethan. "We've wasted enough time."

Ethan returned Cullen's caustic stare. Shea suspected the old man still chafed over his forced retirement. Would he fabricate a hoax to get revenge? After all, he'd still be chief registrar if not for Cullen.

"When will you be back?" Ann reached for Cullen's arm, but a frown from the director stayed her hand.

"Tomorrow. I'll return in time for the Ball."

While they discussed last minute details, Shea turned to Blade, only to find him watching her. She thought he might speak, but the opportunity slipped away when Cheek approached.

"I need to talk to you," he mumbled to Blade. "Outside."

Four

On the way back to the storeroom, Shea stopped by the museum gift shop. Working under klieg lamps was a hot job, and she'd forgotten to pack a sweat band to hold back her long hair. The beaded Indian headbands the museum sold would do just fine.

"Those aren't authentic," a voice said.

She whirled to find Blade standing so close she collided with his broad chest. The faint scent of a woodland glen, of rawhide leather, and the smoke of a hundred council fires caused her head to reel. Or maybe it was his nearness. She could feel his heart beat beneath her hands.

"Not real?" she murmured.

"The headbands."

He had to be at least six foot three or four and all hard, sinewy, gorgeous muscle.

"They were made in Taiwan."

"What?" *The muscles?* "Oh, the headbands."

She could have sworn he said she was the most interesting woman he'd ever met, and he wanted to whisk her away to a mountain cabin. Dragging herself back to reality, she pulled away so fast she nearly fell into a display of frontier bonnets.

"Made in Taiwan?" She flipped the beaded headband over and, sure enough, the words were stamped on the back. "Incredible. Why doesn't the museum sell Native American crafts made by Native Americans?"

"Exactly." He took the band from her and tossed it back into the display box. "I've persuaded the gift shop to stock items made on our Dakota reservation. On consignment. Jewelry. Headbands. Leather wallets. Whatever. The price may be higher, but the quality's better and the money will help fund a clinic for the tribe."

While he talked, Blade led her to a basket sitting on the cashier's counter. He dipped his hand inside and brought out a finely crafted blue and white band and slipped it around her forehead.

"It matches the blue in your eyes. Blue, like prairie flowers."

She didn't realize he'd noticed.

His fingers fumbled with the leather ties. Was he affected by her, too?

His breath caressed her cheek. His lips parted, and she thought he was about to say, "You're the one I've been waiting for."

Instead, he said, "Leather becomes you."

She giggled. Unsuitable for a woman of thirty.

The clerk, who was helping another customer, turned to stare at them. Shea pulled money from her jean pocket.

Blade pushed the bills away. "Until they're sold, they still belong to me. Accept this as a gift from my people."

"Thank you." *What a sweet gesture.* "But I insist." She waved the money at the clerk, who scurried over. "To help convince the museum to stock reservation crafts."

He shot her that heart-stopping smile of his.

God help me. He has the deepest, darkest, brown-velvet eyes.

"Have you seen the new Native American gallery?" he asked, oblivious to her turmoil.

"Actually, I haven't." Anything to distract herself so she could breathe again.

They left the shop and ducked into the new gallery.

"I've been so busy photographing artifacts," she said, surveying the cavernous room, "I haven't had time to see them displayed. Impressive."

They strolled among the collection of Indian history. A full-grown, six-foot-tall-at-the-shoulder stuffed bison, his glass eyes glistening, stood in the center of the gallery. To the left, Pomo baskets, Pueblo pottery, Navajo blankets, Pawnee peace pipes, and beaded medicine bags filled showcase after showcase. A Haida totem depicted some ancient chief's exploits with carved and painted heads of ravens, whales, and bears.

On the right sat a dugout canoe complete with hand-hewn paddle. An eagle feather headdress perched like the mighty bird of prey on a stand next to one of the gallery's floor-to-ceiling windows. A mannequin in the corner wore the knee-length, white leather coat that once belonged to St. Louis fur trader, Manuel Lisa.

Shea peered closer at the coat's tiny embroidered flowers and fluted beads. "Exquisite."

"Thanks," Blade said.

"You restored this? It's such intricate work."

She could imagine his strong hands fashioning an arrow quiver or stretching buffalo hide across a shield, but not needlework. Even after years of accepting dangerous photo assignments to earn the respect of her male colleagues, she chauvinistically envisioned an Indian woman nimbly sewing the delicate flowers.

"For the most part," Blade said, "I'm a painter. Oils. I record the plight of the Indian, the slaughter of the buffalo, and the taking of our land." He pointed to a painting of sad-faced, ragged Indians with bundles on their backs. "Trail of Tears" was engraved on a wooden plaque attached to the large, rustic frame. "Nearly a fourth of the Cherokees on that forced journey died."

Ashamed of how the Indian people had been—still were—treated, she avoided his eyes. "Why'd you agree to help restore the artifacts?"

Protestors had died at Wounded Knee. Native American lobbyists were demanding an accounting of income generated from leased Indian lands. A group in Tennessee staged sit-ins over the public display of the bones of their ancestors. Wouldn't he fight every effort to exploit the Indian?

"I didn't want them restored by someone who cared nothing for their spiritual worth," he said. "An artist's soul goes into his work. These artifacts deserve respect."

She nodded. "Do you live on a reservation?" she asked, changing the difficult subject.

"Sometimes. I do restorations at different museums across the country. And I have a studio in Santa Fe and one on the Dakota reservation. But I don't neglect my duty as a chieftain when I'm not there." He tilted his head and gazed at her. "Now, your turn."

"What?"

"Tell me about yourself. Your work. Your life."

Should she inform him of her strained relationship with her rigid, militaristic father? How he shuffled her off to her grandmother and aunt after her mother died? How his actions instilled an obsessive drive for perfection in her life and work—to get his approval? Or maybe she should tell him she found it difficult to maintain a lasting romantic relationship because her work and its hectic schedule came first. At least she didn't harbor any false illusions about herself.

"I've been a photographer for ten years."

Coward.

"I work as a stringer for various magazines. *Ancient Customs. Europe In A Week. See Scotland. Appalachian Trails.* Others. I'm leaving for Mexico in a few days to do a spread on recently discovered Mayan ruins."

"Sounds exciting. Maybe dangerous."

"Sometimes dangerous. Most of the time it's exciting." She remembered the headhunter tribe she'd lived with for a week in the Amazon jungles. "Always interesting."

He laughed. "You sound like a modern-day female Indiana Jones. How's your boyfriend feel about that?"

"He doesn't like my being gone so much."

A shadow darkened Blade's handsome face.

"But since I broke up with him over a year ago," she said, "it really doesn't matter now, does it?"

The shadow lifted.

They strolled to the far end of the gallery where a Blackfoot tepee made of stripped hides sat. Part of a diorama, the scene featured a glimpse of Indian life in the 1800s. Next to it, a showcase filled with Hopi kachina dolls stared back at her with wide, expressive eyes.

Blade pointed to each one and called their names: Deer Kachina, Black Ogre, Prickly Pear, Mudhead Clown. He motioned at a figure dressed in corn shucks. "That's Homedance Maiden. A fertility spirit."

"Fertility?" she echoed.

His tone lightened, and he relaxed his stance, moving closer to her.

"An Indian brave gives the doll to a maiden on the day he takes her to his tepee."

"Tepee?" she repeated, sounding like a befuddled parrot.

His words slowly sunk in. "Wait a minute. Pueblo Indians didn't live in tepees." She glared at him. "You're teasing me."

With a mischievous grin, he pulled her inside.

His touch caused her heart to hammer like a tom-tom.

He drew her closer. Running his fingers down her arm, he clasped her hand.

Her breath escaped in a ragged gasp. A tingly sensation surged through her.

He wrapped his other hand around her waist and pulled her tight against him.

Oh, god.

His lips brushed her hair, her cheek, making his way to her mouth.

Oh, god. Oh, god.

He kissed at the corner of her lips.

Yes.

Then the other corner.

Yes, yes.

His hold on her tightened.

She could feel his body respond to hers. She didn't think she could stand much more. Any second now she'd lose control, throw her arms around his neck, and devour him.

His lips brushed hers as he moved in for the prize.

She could almost feel them crushing hers before it happened.

Come on, let it happen.

A soft, but insistent, cough outside the tepee interrupted the beginning of something hot and primitive. Reluctantly, Shea held Blade at bay, then pulled away and stepped out of the cone-shaped structure. Ann stood there smiling like the cat that ate a whole flock of canaries.

"Blade," Ann said with an innocent lilt, "Ethan's looking for you. He needs more relics to catalog."

Shea watched as Blade disappeared down the hall. Then she spun toward Ann. "If I have to track you to the ends of the earth," she said through clenched teeth, "I'll make you pay for that."

Ann laughed and linked her arm in Shea's. "How about I buy you lunch instead?"

Good. Shea had questions for her friend.

Five

A lunch crowd packed Giovanni's on The Hill, St. Louis' Italian neighborhood. Shea and Ann scooted into a booth enclosed on three sides by a wooden trellis festooned with artificial grapes. Murals of old Italy painted on cracked plaster walls surrounded them. On the table, scarred from years of service, an empty bottle of Chianti found new life as a candleholder.

Savoring the aroma of simmering pasta sauce and freshly grated Parmesan cheese, Shea ordered baked lasagna, garlic bread, and a Pepsi. Ann chose crab salad spooned onto a bed of bean sprouts and bib lettuce.

"On another one of your diets?" Shea asked.

"Always," Ann responded in a fatalistic tone.

Shea could sympathize. Trekking over the Himalayas in search of Tibet's mythical Yeti, the Swiss Alps following Hannibal's elephant-ridden trail, or any of her other arduous assignments kept Shea in shape. Good thing, since she loved Italian cuisine. And French. And Greek.

No sooner had Ann swallowed her first mouthful of crab when she peppered Shea with questions. "You haven't gone native on me, have you?"

Shea gave her a puzzled look. "What do you mean?"

"The headband."

"Ah, yes. I need it to hold back my hair while I'm working."

"Uh-huh. What's going on with you and Blade? Not that I blame you. What a hunk."

Great. Caught making out in a tepee, no less. "Nothing. We only met this morning."

A grin spread across Ann's face. "Seemed awfully friendly for strangers. I think I saw smoke coming out the top of the tepee."

"Forget that. What's with you and Cullen Gerard? You didn't mention him when you hired me at lunch yesterday."

"What? Nothing. We're colleagues." Ann clammed up.

Standing her ground while photographing a charging rhino on the Serengeti had prepared Shea for moments like this. She could outlast her friend.

Dishes clattered. People chatted. Waiters waited.

Ann caved. "All right. I meant to tell you, but you've only been back in town two days."

"So, tell me now."

Ann lowered her voice. "You can't breathe this to a soul."

"Breathe what?"

Ann looked as if she were about to choke on crab meat. "We're...lovers."

Big news flash. Shea suspected as much, what with Ann's adoring gaze every time Cullen spoke. But that's not the information she was fishing for. "Why the cloak and dagger? Is he married?"

"No, no, no. Nothing like that. If anyone knew about us, it might jeopardize my appointment to the Guggenheim. He's recommending me."

Ann's green eyes grew blissful.

"Cullen is respected, his work renowned. He's held important positions at the Museum of Natural History in Boston, the Founding Fathers of Philadelphia, and the Denver Archives of Western Expansion. I've always dreamed of running one of those larger museums."

"Isn't that how the 'ol' boy' system works?" Shea couldn't keep disdain from her voice. "I've hit the glass ceiling so many times, the Flatheads have accepted me into their tribe."

Ann patted the top of Shea's head and laughed, but her tone implied scorn for the system, not mirth.

"Cullen thinks the Guggenheim's board of directors might suspect friends as bedmates. We are...more than friends, but that has nothing to do with his recommendation." Ann hesitated. "It's for the good of the Missouri Westward Museum, too. He can raise more money from patrons, mostly wives of rich businessmen, if he's unattached."

Maybe Cullen did have Ann's best interest at heart. Having worked at so many different institutions, he knew how the system operated. Their secret alliance appeared innocent, even romantic. Still, the deception, following on the heels of Ethan's claim of an artifact fraud, worried Shea. If the lance was a forgery, would the authorities suspect a conspiracy?

"So tell me how you can't live without him." Shea was glad to see her friend make room in her life for a relationship.

Look who's talking. Miss I'm-Too-Busy-With-My-Work-To-Get-Involved McKenna.

Woman cannot live by professional accolades alone.

Grandmother McKenna's words echoed in Shea's ears. After the car wreck that took her mother's life, Shea had gone to live with Gram and Aunt Kathryn in St. Louis. Maybe it was the accident or maybe the military life her little family led moving from base to base, but her father—Major Andrew McKenna—had found it difficult to handle his moody, belligerent teenage daughter. So he shipped her off to Gram, who considered it her duty to marry off her daughter and granddaughter to nice men. So far, Gram had failed on both counts, not that Kathryn and Shea gave her much help.

But Shea could revel in Ann's love life.

"Come on. Give it up," Shea coaxed. "Is he romantic? A good lover? Kinky? What?"

Struggling to keep a straight face, Ann ignored Shea's questions. "Cullen rescues floundering foundations. Not that the Missouri museum is in trouble."

"That's not what Cullen said," Shea corrected. "He implied John Franklin ran the museum into the ground." *Otherwise, why hire a troubleshooter like Cullen Gerard?*

"When our previous director died, the board brought in Cullen. The first thing he did was clean house. It devastated Ethan when Cullen retired him."

What a sweet, gut-wrenching euphemism. Ethan was "retired," not fired.

"Do you think Ethan would claim the lance is a forgery to cause trouble for Cullen?"

"Ethan can be grouchy, but he doesn't mean anything by it. I can't imagine him being vengeful. Besides, if the lance proves authentic, he'd be the one looking foolish."

"He mentioned something about 'cannibalizing' artifacts."

"What you have are Indians refurbishing genuine pieces of their history with dated material. Someone might use scraps to make a new item, but how could you tell?"

Shea had formed a picture of Blade as an honorable, caring man, a perfect leader for his people. The role of forger didn't fit. "Has this ever been done?"

"There's a fellow in Maine—Greene's his name—who turns out copies that fool the experts. Last year Sotheby's sold a beaded medicine pouch to a lady in Belgium for $10,000. Greene saw it in their catalog and recognized the item as his own work. He even produced photographs taken at various stages of construction to verify his claim."

"Then Greene hadn't intended to fool anyone?"

"An honest artisan doesn't want the market flooded with forgeries any more than museums or auction houses." Ann quirked a brow. "Can you imagine Sotheby's embarrassment? The woman was so taken with Greene's designs, however, she ordered two more pouches at a price of $300 each."

Shea shook her head. "I had no idea the market for Indian artifacts was so healthy in Europe."

"Anything to do with the American Indian is hot." Ann blotted her lips with a napkin. "A 200-year-old sun-bleached buckskin vest with colored beads and quills commands a price of $30,000. Worn with a silk blouse and Calvin Klein jeans, it's the play togs of the glitterati."

Would Blade sell out his people? This didn't agree with his talk of a medical center. Or did it?

"Blade mentioned something about a clinic. I guess it doesn't matter where the money comes from."

"It's a sad situation. The nearest facility is sixty miles from the reservation. Their mortality rate is tragic. Blade and his men restore artifacts to raise money. And the museum is donating a portion of the proceeds from the Patrons Ball."

A worried look darkened Ann's face. "The items are only out of the museum when they're being repaired by Blade and his men. I suppose they could sell the relics and replace them with forgeries."

Shea laid down her fork. She'd lost her appetite. "How are they stored at the workshop?"

"The Indians never leave the relics alone for a minute. They work in shifts. One of them even sleeps there." Ann drained her iced tea. "Why don't we drop by on our way back to the museum? The workshop's in the park. You can get a look at the setup."

Whatever their reason for visiting the Indians' workplace, Shea looked forward to seeing Blade again.

Ann shook her head. "I still don't believe there's been a falsification. Maybe Cullen's right. Maybe Ethan's too old for this profession."

Or maybe they'll find evidence supporting Ethan's claim. If so, the forgery happened while the lance was in Blade's care.

Shea's enthusiasm for visiting the workshop faded.

Six

On their way to the Indians' workshop, Ann asked, "How's your aunt Kathryn? And Gram? Gram's so sweet. I never get to see her when you're away. I miss her. She's almost like *my* grandmother."

"She'd gladly volunteer for the job," Shea replied. "Of course, that would mean she'd try to marry you off to every Tom, Dick, and Cullen who came down the pike."

Ann laughed. "You know that saying originated here in St. Louis at the 1904 World's Fair."

"What? Tom, Dick, and Cullen? Is Cullen that old?"

"Stop it. I mean the phrase 'came down the pike.'"

"Yeah?"

Shea knew the phrase's origin, but Ann liked to show off her repertoire of odd pieces of information whenever an opportunity presented itself. No longer a docent at the museum, as curator she had little chance to regale tourists with her knowledge of Missouri history. She was limited now to displaying her talent at citing historical tidbits for donors at the Patrons Ball or for a trapped friend riding with her in a car.

Ann eyed Shea. "But you already know that, don't you?"

"Refresh my memory."

Shea had no intention of raining on her friend's parade. Besides, if she kept Ann busy, she wouldn't be asking Shea probing questions about her rendezvous in the tepee with Blade.

"The Pike was a mile-long stretch at the Fair that featured

attractions like exotic locations and historical events," Ann said. "The supernatural. Side shows. Carnival-type oddities. So if someone said, 'It was the strangest thing that ever came down the Pike,' then it was pretty strange."

"Some of the blind dates Gram has set me up with have been pretty doggone strange," Shea said. "She once matched me with a forty-year-old accountant. The only son of one of her Mah Jong friends."

Ann pulled into a paved lot next to a single-story building on museum grounds. "Nothing wrong with a forty-year-old accountant."

"No, there isn't. But I was only nineteen and he still lived with his mother. Gram first matched him with Aunt Kathryn. Kathryn dumped him. I figure if she doesn't want him, why should I?"

"I see your point."

"So if you wish to join the McKenna clan and have Gram pick out a husband for you, be my guest."

That would be a good deal for Shea. She could concentrate her own efforts on a certain tall, dark, and gorgeous Indian if Gram busied herself playing match-maker for Ann.

They parked and entered the workshop. If Shea thought Blade would be glad to see her, she was mistaken. The inscrutable expression clouding his face surprised her, as if their amorous encounter never happened.

"Hello again," she said, hoping she'd misread his frown.

He nodded distractedly and glanced around the room at his artisans. Three men diligently worked at individual tables. Brushes, picks, needles, scissors, small hammers, and jars of glue lay within reach. The place reeked of cleaning fluids and old leather.

Besides overhead florescent lights and individual goose-neck lamps, a line of windows on three walls provided illumination for the Indians as well as a view of the surrounding park and museum. Arms crossed over his chest, Cheek Larson leaned against a workbench in a far corner.

Shea glanced back at Blade.

He refused to look at her.

The heat of embarrassment crept up her neck. Turning away, she took a deep breath to calm her injured pride.

Okay, Shea, think rationally. Why would he snub you?

She'd popped in unexpectedly, startled him.

Then give him a chance to recover.

Recover from what? How had she upset him?

Maybe there was more to his discomfort than getting caught romancing the museum photographer.

"Hello, Blade," she tried again.

He returned her greeting without looking at her. Shea glanced at Ann. Her friend arched a puzzled brow.

"Blade," Ann said, as if nothing was amiss, "why don't you introduce Shea to your men and show us what they're working on?"

Feelings bruised, Shea preferred to make a hasty retreat. But then Blade would know he'd wounded her. That was the last thing she wanted.

He led them to the first worktable. "This is Elk Horn. He's repairing a Cheyenne crow, a dance bustle once worn by Dog Soldiers."

A short, stocky man sporting a long gray ponytail and wearing jeans and a purple-flowered calico shirt nodded at them, then returned to his work. He polished the antique brass hawk bells and French brass sequins that secured the bustle's feathers. He then fanned them in a circle and began to replace any that were damaged.

"What kind of feathers are those?" Ann asked.

"Hawk," Elk Horn said, his weathered face pinched and puckered like a dried apple-head doll. "Some turkey."

"Beautiful. Aren't the Dog Soldiers Cheyenne? Were there Sioux Dog Soldiers?"

"They were one of six Cheyenne military societies established in the 1830s. To resist the expansion of the white man into Indian Territory." He seemed to warm to the opportunity to talk of his history. "They intermarried with the Sioux."

Ann bent for a closer look at the dance bustle. "Beautiful work, Elk Horn."

He puffed out his chest. "Thank you. The Dog Soldier society has re-established itself at the Northern Cheyenne Indian Reservation in Montana and the Cheyenne-Arapaho Reservation in Oklahoma. I've been commissioned to make their bustles."

"That's wonderful," Ann said.

Shea remembered reading Indian activist Russell Means' speech of 1980, *For America to Live, Europe Must Die*. She wondered whether the military society had been established as an honorary order or were the Indians gathering forces to wage war against, as Means states, "cultural genocide"?

Blade rubbed the back of his neck and glanced away as Ann continued to ask Elk Horn questions about his restoration methods. The chieftain seemed anxious to finish the tour and hurriedly introduced the next worker.

"This is Billy Quintella." An Arapaho blanket woven in blacks, golds, and yellows depicting a setting sun lay across the young man's lap.

"That's beautiful." Shea smiled at Billy and his T-shirt emblazoned with a picture of four Indians sitting horseback on a ridge. The caption read, "Homeland Security."

He ducked his head. "I'm just spot cleaning it. All the artistic work is original. But I can weave," he added. "And paint. And carve. And string beads, hair pipes, and river shells."

"Well, you're doing an excellent job. The colors are so vibrant."

A broad smile spread across his ruddy face. Blade remained stoic.

On their way to the next workbench, they passed a closed door. Ann reached for the knob. "What's in here?"

Blade grabbed it first and held the door shut. "Whoever guards the relics at night sleeps there. Just a cot and some personal items."

His agitation filled Shea with further misgivings. Was the war lance a fake? Had they interrupted the men in the act of forging artifacts? Maybe they'd stashed the true relics behind the closed door.

As curator, Ann had unrestricted access to anything on the grounds. She surprised Shea by letting the affront pass.

Next, Blade herded them toward a mountain of a man hunched over a shield made of buffalo hide. "This is Four Bears of the Cheyenne and Sioux."

The big Indian grunted as he continued to dry-brush the painting of a buffalo's head on the shield's leather top. Long black braids hung over massive shoulders clothed in a brown calico shirt. His profile looked as if someone had carved it in granite, hard and unyielding.

"Very nice," Shea said.

He ignored her.

Great, now she had two Indians mad at her. What had she done?

After an awkward moment filled with what Shea interpreted as controlled animosity from Four Bears, Ann dragged her toward the door that led outside.

"Got to go," Ann said. "I'm sure Ethan has more artifacts for Shea to photograph. See you all at the Ball tomorrow night."

Shea glanced over her shoulder at Blade, who was talking now to Cheek.

The chieftain's glower had morphed into a look of quiet desperation.

Seven

Stung and confused by Blade's coldness toward her, Shea remained mute as she and Ann walked from the workshop, across the lawn, to the museum's back door.

Inside the vestibule, Ann said, "Shea, I—about Blade—"

"Forget it." Shea interrupted. "My fault. I read too much into his attention. He was just flirting. Having a little fun."

"He was rude."

"He's history."

They high-fived each other.

"Okay. I've got relics to photograph." Shea's voice carried a little too much bravado.

She spun on a heel and headed for the basement stairs, leaving Ann to iron out last minute details for the Ball. Upon entering the storeroom, she found Ethan bent studiously over his workbench scribbling notes.

"I'm back," she said to his hunched shoulders.

"Ummm," he mumbled.

Snubbed again.

Okay, McKenna, finish your work and get the heck out of Dodge. St. Louis doesn't love you anymore.

She set up her next shot and pushed Blade from her thoughts. Not an easy feat, considering she was hip deep in Indian relics. An hour later, the concentration her work demanded kicked in, and she forgot all about the handsome chieftain and his broad shoulders. Mostly.

Ann sent a deli deliveryman down with roast beef sandwiches and a message that she was too busy to join them for dinner. An eternity dragged by until Ethan glanced at his pocket watch, tapped its face, and turned to Shea.

"What time do you have?"

She arose from the beaded moccasins, medicine bag, and feathered fan she was arranging for a fantastic shot and glanced at her wristwatch. "It's midnight." Moaning, she stretched her aching back. "My, how time flies when you're having fun."

The attempt at humor was lost on Ethan.

"Do you think Miss Scott's still here?" he said.

She peered into the camera's viewfinder and adjusted the lens to get the right depth of field. "Could be."

"I have an idea that might tell us who switched the lance."

Shea shook her head. The old man was like a terrier digging out a rat; he refused to let go of his suspicions. Cullen and Cheek had flown to Santa Fe, but he'd still have Blade to contend with.

"I have more relics to photograph."

Blade's attraction to her proved superficial, demonstrated by his callousness at the workshop. Still, she wanted to keep track of what was going on with the lance, even if it meant facing him again.

Torn by conflicting goals, she asked, "Want me to come with you?"

Ethan jutted out his chin. "That won't be necessary, Miss McKenna. I don't need a wet nurse."

Men.

Can't live with 'em. Can't live without 'em. Can't wring their necks.

𝕽

Shea brought the final shot of a Cheyenne necklace made of sun-bleached porcupine quills and blue beads into focus. Wiping her damp palms on a hand towel, she picked up the camera's cable release and positioned her thumb on the shutter button.

"As they say in Hollywood, you're only as good as your last picture."

Lucrative assignments could come her way if the businessmen and women attending the Patrons Ball were impressed with her efforts.

Finished, she carefully picked up the delicate piece of jewelry. Guessing it once graced a Cheyenne maiden's neck, temptation overwhelmed her. She held it at her throat and admired her reflection in a brass spittoon sitting on a shelf. The choker complimented the blue and white headband she'd bought in the museum's gift shop.

The notion drew her thoughts back to Blade.

Forget him. He's old news.

Returning the necklace to its velvet bed, she checked the time again. An hour had passed since Ethan went to see Ann. He'd instructed her to photograph only the cataloged artifacts. Nothing more. But they were on a tight schedule, and she wasn't eager to incite Cullen's wrath if she missed tomorrow's deadline.

Tired and hungry, she closed her eyes and massaged her temples. A doozie of a headache galloped across her forehead like a herd of wild horses. She glanced at Ethan's stool. His green tweed jacket with its leather elbow patches still hung across the back. He must not have gone home yet.

Home. Not a bad idea. A hot bath awaited her. A glass of wine. A comfortable bed.

She unscrewed the camera from its tripod. Tomorrow was another day. She'd rise early and start on whatever Ethan had ready.

Packing her camera bag, she flung it over her shoulder and grabbed his jacket. She'd take it to Ann's office and bid them a good evening. Besides, she was curious to know what Ethan had discovered about the lance.

Switching off the storeroom lights, she stepped into a dimly lit hallway and pulled the door shut behind her. It locked automatically.

She'd never worked this late before and didn't expect the museum to be so dark. Sparse light spilled from the supply room at the end of the hall. The light flickered.

"Ethan? Ethan, is that you?"

When no one answered, she hurried the opposite direction toward the stairway that would lead to Ann's office on the second floor. She turned left at a cross corridor. Then froze.

Someone stood in the shadows against the opposite wall.

Shea remained still, holding her breath to mask her anxiety. The person didn't speak or move. She exhaled slowly, then took another breath, waiting for the figure to identify himself and relieve her fears.

Sounds around her magnified. A clock ticking nearby thundered in her ears. A faucet dripped. Something tiny scurried in the dark.

Gathering her nerve, she spoke around the lump in her throat. "Mr. Brumley?"

No answer.

Taller than Ethan, the hump-backed figure's pale face remained hidden beneath a tumult of dark straggly hair, the rest of him lost in the shadows.

"Who's there?" Her words sounded more like a plea than a demand. She pressed against the hall's unyielding stone wall for support. Its cool surface and her situation sent chills up her spine. "Answer me. Please."

You're jumping at bogeymen, Shea. It's just a guard patrolling the building.

Or one of the Indians.

Or Cheek Larson.

That thought caused the hair on the back of her neck to spike until she remembered he'd flown to Santa Fe with Cullen.

The knowledge didn't relieve her apprehension. The mysterious figure waited, silent, unmoving. If he belonged in the museum—to guard it, to clean it, to work on last minute details for the Patrons Ball—why didn't he answer?

Shea's heart pounded like a sledgehammer. She couldn't return to the storeroom. The door locked behind her, and she had no key.

Her only chance?

Run.

Run!

Her legs refused to move. Adjusting the camera bag slung across her shoulder, she edged forward.

The figure shivered and groped at his hunched back.

Gasping, she halted, her heart pounding faster.

She slid one foot forward.

He followed.

This was no good. Think. Think.

She scrutinized him more closely, but remained still.

He did the same.

She raised her hand to her forehead.

The intruder mimicked her every move.

When recognition dawned, she exhaled in relief. "You're a real hoot, Shea."

You've just spent ten minutes scaring yourself to death with your own reflection.

She frowned at her distorted image in one of the museum's empty glass showcases. Clad in black jeans and T-shirt, the camera bag thrown across her back, she'd mistaken herself for some monstrous fiend. She needed a new look.

Sucking in courage with a gulp of air, she bounded up the basement steps.

On the main floor, she scuttled swiftly down the dim hallways. Moonlight streamed in the gallery windows and cast streaks that resembled bony fingers onto the marble walls. Statues of dead statesmen frowned down at her from granite pedestals as though angry their peace had been disturbed. Portraits of pale ladies dressed in silks and crinolines peeked from the shadows.

Shea thought she saw two dark figures by the entrance to the Native American gallery, but when she rubbed her eyes they had vanished.

"You're imagining things again." Her voice had turned high-pitched and accusative.

Quickening her step, she vaulted up the winding stairs to the second level. This hallway was well lit. She tried Ann's office but found the door locked, its frosted window dark.

"I'm here all by myself," she said in disbelief.

Her words echoed down the corridor. Nothing was scarier than an empty museum at night, except maybe, a graveyard.

"Great, *now* I feel better."

"Who's there?" a deep, raspy voice rumbled from the direction she'd come. A man wearing gray coveralls and carrying a mop rounded the corner. She sighed with relief at the sight of a museum custodian.

"I'm Shea McKenna." She flashed her identification badge. "Has Ann Scott left?"

"Don't know." He shuffled past her, smelling of disinfectant and glass cleaner, and headed for a utility cart at the end of the hall. "She was here earlier, when I was emptying waste baskets. I remember 'cause some old guy was looking for her."

"Mr. Brumley," Shea said.

"Whatever. Forgot my mop. Had to go back to the supply room to get it." He eyed Ann's dark office. "Guess they left while I was in the basement. You must've just missed 'em."

The janitor had caused the supply room light to flicker. It had been Ann and Ethan by the new gallery. And her own image reflected in the glass showcase. That accounted for all the murderous fiends her imagination had dredged up.

"Thanks," she read the name embroidered on his coveralls, "Joe."

Making her way to the entry foyer, she bid good night to a guard as he opened the front door, then locked it behind her. When she switched the heavy camera bag to the other shoulder, she discovered Ethan's coat still draped across her arm. Turning, she rapped on the museum's glass door.

The guard reopened it a crack. "Yes, ma'am?"

"Did you see Ann Scott and Ethan Brumley leave?"

"No, ma'am. They could've left by the rear exit, though. Doors are locked, but Miss Scott knows the alarm code."

Strange Ethan *and* Ann would leave without telling her. She'd have to return his coat in the morning.

"You parked far away?" the guard asked.

"Right there."

She pointed to a burgundy Trailblazer nosed in at the curb. A wide expanse of lawn shadowed by giant oaks lay between her and the circle drive. Turn-of-the-century streetlamps rimmed the boulevard, their eerie glow haloed in the thick summer haze.

"I'll keep an eye out 'til you get in your car," he said.

"Thanks."

The Blazer's engine fluttered, died, surged once more, and took hold. She backed out of the parking space, honked another "thank you" at the guard, and circled the museum. Ann's red MG was nowhere in sight. Only four vehicles remained in the rear parking area, probably belonging to the guards and the janitorial team.

As the custodian said, she must've just missed Ann and Ethan.

Eight

"Oatmeal," the voice shouted.

Groggy from only five hours sleep, Shea reconciled oatmeal with her dream about a handsome Indian chief. He was just about to—

"Oatmeal!"

Aunt Kathryn? What was she doing in the tepee with Blade and Shea?

The third shout of "oatmeal" catapulted Shea out of bed as efficiently as an alarm clock—which she'd forgotten to set once again. When Aunt Kathryn, who lived with Gram in the huge old house at Number Two Aberdeen Place, began breakfast, she'd holler the morning menu out the back door. Living in the carriage house behind the ancestral home, Shea would shower, dress, and join her grandmother and aunt in their kitchen. Due to her travel schedule, she didn't see her family often and cherished this ritual.

"Morning Gram." Shea bent and kissed her grandmother, seated at a richly-carved oblong table in the center of the kitchen.

Gram patted Shea's hand. "Good morning, dear."

Shea deposited her purse and camera bag on a counter and ambled over to the refrigerator. Opening its door, she pulled out a cold bottle of Pepsi-Cola.

"I wish you'd eat a more nourishing breakfast," Kathryn said.

"Good morning to you too, Katie," Shea responded, using a name her aunt disliked. Their good-natured teasing began the day Shea moved in. "I'm only in town a few days," she added. "Is this going to be our morning routine? Me having my usual Pepsi for breakfast and you trying to stuff healthy food down me?"

Grinning, she toasted her aunt with the Pepsi bottle and took a long swig. The cola's sharp bite burned her throat and sent a wake-up call to her brain.

Kathryn stuck out her tongue but couldn't quite hide the smile pulling at the corner of her mouth.

"Oh, yeah, real mature," Shea said. "You're forty-nine Kathryn, dearest. Deal with it."

Shea hoped she looked as good when she was that age. Short, sand-colored hair skimmed her aunt's wrinkle-free face as she gave the steaming oatmeal a final stir. Still in jogging shorts from her morning run, Kathryn's lean thigh muscles rippled beneath tanned skin that glowed with good health. If it depended on eating oatmeal for the rest of her life, Shea could kiss good health goodbye.

"Yeah, well, this forty-nine-year-old ran the Boston Marathon last year. Remember when you could run the mile in seven minutes?"

"I can still do a respectable ten. Nine, if there's a good reason to push myself." The bulls at Pamplona had been a good enough reason. She'd found it difficult to get a printable photo with a 2,000-pound raging bovine barreling down on her. A well-placed hoof left bruises on her derriere.

Kathryn's grin widened. "Twenty bucks says you can't beat me around the track at Wash U, Sunday."

"After church," Gram chimed in.

"You're on." Goading her aunt, Shea swigged another mouthful of Pepsi. Rivalry with Kathryn brought out her competitive nature.

Kathryn shook her head and raised a ladle of dripping oatmeal over Shea. "Oatmeal's good for you. Want some?"

Shea ducked behind Gram. "None for me, thanks."

"Girls. Girls. Please. Conduct yourselves like the genteel ladies you are." Gram could barely keep a straight face.

"Truce?" Kathryn said, offering her hand.

"Truce." Shea reached out, but before she could clasp her aunt's hand, Kathryn jerked it back and thumbed her nose at Shea.

"That is soooo yesterday, Kathryn. You're showing your age again."

Kathryn grabbed Shea and hugged her. "When'd you get back? I've missed you."

"Day before yesterday. You and Gram were out somewhere. I called Ann Scott for lunch. She's got a tight deadline and staff out with a virus going 'round. So, she commandeered me to photograph Indian relics."

Turning Shea loose, Kathryn dipped scoops of oatmeal into two crockery bowls. She deposited one in front of Gram and sat down with the other.

"Thank you, dear," Gram said and turned to Shea. "So, have you finished photographing the Indian what-knots?"

Shea smiled at her grandmother's choice of words. Although a patron of the History Museum, at times Gram seemed unconcerned how her donations were spent. The McKenna fortune, inherited from an enterprising, frugal Scottish ancestor, had disappeared after it fell into her generous hands. If it weren't for Kathryn's lectures, Shea's photography, and the money her father sent, the spry, eighty-five-year-old matriarch would've been forced to live a life far removed from "genteel." All that remained of Margaret "Peggy" McKenna's legacy was the family home on Aberdeen Place across from Forest Park.

"I have a few more relics to photograph for the patron's books," Shea said.

Although she was dying to tell them about the possibility of a forged artifact, Cullen had issued strict instructions not to tell *anyone*. At least not until the relic was verified—or not—Monday.

"I'll still have shots to take for the catalog, but there's no time limit on those," she said, hoping her voice didn't betray her secret. "Done or not, I'll be leaving on assignment for Mexico in three days."

"You're leaving again? Already?" Kathryn questioned.

"Darling, you've only just returned," Gram said. "We hardly ever get to see you anymore."

"I know. I'm sorry. I miss you guys too."

It was true. Shea missed her family when she was on assignment. But after a few weeks at home, the mundane set in. By then, she was ready to climb the walls. She cherished Gram and Kathryn, but she cherished her freedom, too.

Gram slipped a Damask napkin from beneath her silverware and laid it across the lap of her faded lavender-flowered dress. With her other hand, she fiddled with a strand of pearls around her neck, the last remnant of a brimming jewelry box not sold off.

"My goodness, are you doing all that work at the museum alone?"

"No. I'm stuck down in the dusty catacombs with a man three times my age. Ethan Brumley, the registrar. Why can't historians be young and dashing like Indiana Jones? Or like the real globe-trotting archeologist Richard Halliburton. Now there was a hunk."

"He died before you were born," Kathryn said from the opposite side of the table. "Heck, he died before I was born."

"Don't rain on my parade, Kathryn. He's the reason I'm in this line of work."

"You have a crush on a dead man. You need to get out more."

"Well..."

Shea would like to discuss Blade's strange behavior with her aunt but not in front of Gram. Upon rising this morning, she'd decided to get him alone and give him a chance to explain himself. It was the fair thing to do. She could use her aunt's thoughts on the matter.

Kathryn raised her eyes to Shea. "Well—what?"

"Well, there's this handsome Indian chief."

"Details," Kathryn said. "I need details."

"Tall. Broad shoulders. Long black hair with braided forelocks. Dark eyes. Muscular build. Feathers. Your average Native American."

"Does he have a brother?"

"Kathryn, you're drooling in your oatmeal. What happened to the independent I-don't-need-a-man women's libber? You burned your bra in the '60s."

"That was my bra she burned," Gram said. "She was only twelve."

Through the years, Gram had instructed her granddaughter in proper, ladylike behavior, while Kathryn shouted feminist slogans. Upon reaching eighteen, Shea moved into the renovated carriage house out back in search of an opinion of her own. Her trips to godforsaken corners of the earth on photo shoots nullified the need to move farther away.

"There are certain things men are good for," Kathryn admitted. "Do I have to explain the birds and the bees to you again?"

"I don't think so. It got pretty hot and heavy in the tepee."

"Good heavens, Shea, are there no local men for you to date?" Gram asked. "If you move to a reservation, I'll never see you. Not that I see much of you now."

"Shush, Mom. Shea has more to tell."

"That's all I'm saying for now." Shea signaled a close to the subject with another swig of Pepsi. She'd talk to Kathryn later, when Gram wasn't around.

"Speaking of local men." Kathryn retrieved a jar of wheat germ from the refrigerator. Returning to the table, she heaped a spoonful of the brown granules atop her oatmeal. "Philip Ross called."

Shea frowned. "Philip doesn't resemble Indiana Jones in the least. And he's dull as—as—wheat germ."

Kathryn stopped shaking the granules into her bowl. "It's nothing to me whether you return his call, but he mentioned something about the Patrons Ball tonight."

"I'm already going. By myself. By choice. I suffered through two uneventful dates with Philip to please Gram and her matchmaking endeavors."

Kathryn winked at Shea. "Better she hound you to the altar than me."

Not the least bit contrite, Gram reached over and patted Shea's hand again.

"Nothing clicked between us," Shea continued. "No fireworks. No romantic music. Not even a murmur. The 'Night of the Living Dead' would be an accurate description of our last date."

Gram scowled. "I fail to understand why certain members in this family avoid marriage like it was the Black Plague. Shea, you're already thirty. And Kathryn. At forty-nine you're certainly past your childbearing years. If it weren't for your brother and Elizabeth—may she rest in peace—I'd have no grandchildren at all."

Even though Gram was Presbyterian, she crossed herself. Mentioning Shea's dead mother brought out the old woman's Scottish flair for the superstitious.

"Don't start on me, Mom," Kathryn said in mock annoyance and pointed her spoon at Gram. "By the way, I won't be home for lunch. I have to give a lecture on 'Women's Roles in Different Cultures' at the college in Cape."

"Cape Girardeau's quite a distance. Will you be back in time for the Ball?" Gram asked. "Or shall I take a cab?"

"It's a two hour drive to Cape and two hours back. Three hours to give the lecture, answer questions, and eat lunch with the faculty. I'll be back in time to shower, dress, and take you to the Ball."

"Thank you, dear."

"I'm going with Jonathan Wakefield. I'm sure he'll be glad to drive you over, too."

The news of her daughter's impending date brightened Gram's smile. She trilled a pleased, "Oh, that nice history professor from Washington University?"

"I knew that would make your day," Kathryn said with an air of resignation.

Shea fluttered her eyelashes at her aunt, who stifled a chuckle. Margaret McKenna wouldn't be satisfied until they were married and had started a family of their own.

"Oh, Katie." Shea's teasing voice took on a falsetto tone. "Jonathan Wakefield. Now there's marriage material. Head of the history department at Wash U. Broad shoulders. Barrel chest. Squat physique. He looks like a cute bulldog, don't you think, Katie?"

Kathryn smirked at Shea. "And as Jonathan's assistant, Philip will be coming too, of course, whether you're his date or not."

Shea stood up. "I hope the four of you have a wonderful time."

Gram turned to Shea. "Kathryn will be away for lunch. Will you be dining with me, dear?"

"Love to, Gram, but I'll probably have to work straight through lunch and dinner."

Which reminded Shea, a storeroom full of Indian artifacts awaited her. Not to mention a hectic schedule, disgruntled, enigmatic Indians, and a forged war lance. With forced enthusiasm, she scooped up her purse and camera equipment and dashed out the back door.

"Gotta go."

Nine

Flashing lights accosted Shea as she parked behind the museum. Four police cars, the coroner's station wagon, and a Crime Scene Unit's van angled in at the curb. CSU investigators searched an area cordoned off by yellow tape tied from tree to tree. The park's mounted patrol held gawkers at a safe distance. A speculative murmur ran through the crowd.

Shea retrieved her camera bag and purse from the Blazer's back seat and slung them over her shoulder. What was going on? Had there been a carjacking? A hit-and-run? A drug deal gone bad? Trying to see what all the commotion was about, she headed for the museum's back door at a slow pace. A uniformed officer blocked the way.

"No press until the forensic people are finished," he said.

"I work here." She dug through her purse, pulled out her I. D. badge, and clipped it to a belt loop. "What happened?"

"You work last night?"

"Yes."

"Just a minute." He pressed a button on his walkie-talkie.

"Yeah," a voice responded.

"It's O'Reilly. Got a—" He turned to her. "What's the name?"

"Shea McKenna."

"Got a Shea McKenna. Museum photographer. Says she worked last night."

"I'll send Wolkalski down to get her."

"What's going on?" she asked O'Reilly.

"The lieutenant will let you know."

"But—"

"Lieutenant Jansen."

While she waited, Shea glanced back at the cordoned area. Dr. Mary Case, St. Louis' Chief Medical Examiner, and an assistant were bent over what appeared to be a discarded bag of rumpled clothes. A CSU investigator circled the unkempt form and snapped pictures. As he moved out of Shea's line of sight, she realized what she saw. Stunned, she staggered backwards against the museum door.

It was Ethan Brumley's broken and bloodied body.

A feathered war lance pierced his chest, pinning him to the ground.

𝕽

Officer Wolkalski ushered Shea into Ann's office. Her friend sat at a desk shredding damp tissue. Mascara tears puddled at the edge of Ann's eyes. A man wearing a St. Louis Cardinals jacket and baseball cap rested a hip on the edge of her desk.

"Lieutenant, this lady says she's a photographer for the museum," Wolkalski said. "Uh, what's your name, again?"

Still shaken, she mumbled her name and rushed to wrap an arm around Ann. "Will someone tell me what's going on?"

"Oh, Shea," Ann moaned.

"Lieutenant Jansen. Homicide," the Cardinals fan said. "Have a seat."

He motioned to a chair next to the desk.

"Please, what—"

Jansen cut her off. "You know an Ethan Brumley?"

The sight of the war lance protruding from Ethan's chest flashed before her eyes.

"Yes. When—how?"

The questions caught in her throat, but they raced like mice through a maze in her head. Who would want to kill the frail little man? And why? Surely not over one supposedly forged artifact? Maybe if she'd looked for him sooner last night...

She took a deep breath.

Regaining her composure, Shea asked again, "Please, could someone tell me what happened?"

"Take a seat," Jansen repeated.

She sat.

He took a pack of Marlboros from his jacket pocket, placed one between his lips, and flipped open a lighter. His movements were slow, deliberate. Except for Ann's sniffles, the room was quiet, the activity outside muffled by the museum's stone walls. He hadn't lit the cigarette yet, but Shea could smell stale smoke on him from previous encounters with the weed. It didn't help her nausea.

She glanced at Ann, but her friend continued to shred tissue onto the desktop. Was Jansen's silence a ploy to unnerve them, to get her or Ann to say something incriminating? Ann appeared to be on the verge of collapse.

Jansen's lighter blazed into life.

"No!" Ann stopped crying long enough to wave a tissue at him. "No smoking in the museum."

Frowning, he shoved the unlit cigarette back into his pocket.

"Who'd want to kill Ethan?" Shea tried again.

Ann sobbed and reached for a fresh tissue. Despite Jansen's instructions, Shea hurried to calm her friend.

"I was just about to ask that question when you waltzed in," he said. "Where were you last night, Miss Scott?"

"Working late. Here, in my office."

"Me too," Shea said, "along with Ethan. In the storeroom."

"Doing what?"

"Photographing Native American artifacts."

Ann nodded and blew her nose. "They'll go on display tonight in the new gallery. We were rushed for time and working late."

Ann's brows furrowed. Shea wondered if she struggled with her promise to Cullen to keep the lance's provenance a secret until after the Ball. She, however, harbored no such loyalty. A man had died. The Ball would have to take a back seat.

"Ethan suspected that a Sioux war lance owned by the museum had been forged." She related the previous day's events. "Ann's office was dark," she finished, "so I left."

"Miss Scott told you she was going home?" Jansen stared at them with wide-set, bulging eyes. He reminded her of a grouper she'd photographed off the coast of Ecuador last year.

"Well, no. I didn't actually see her before I left. She was already gone."

"You saw her leave?"

"No, I just assumed because her office was locked…"

He focused on Ann. "Then you were the last person to see Brumley alive."

"I didn't see him at all," Ann said.

What? Shea struggled to keep her mouth shut.

"I haven't seen Ethan since yesterday morning," Ann continued, "when we were all in the conference room. I was making arrangements for the Ball tonight—" She gasped. A manicured hand still clutching a soggy tissue flew to her mouth. "The Ball. What will Cullen say?"

Ann's demeanor surprised Shea. But neither had ever experienced violent death on such personal, in-your-face terms. Later, when she had time to fully visualize the murder scene, she, too, might crumble in a blubbering heap.

"Who's Cullen?" Jansen asked.

"Cullen Gerard," Ann replied. "Director of the Gateway Historical Society."

"Is he here?"

"No, not yet."

"Sorry to contradict you."

They turned as Cullen entered the room escorted by another officer who identified him to Jansen.

Ann lunged for the tear-drenched tissues dotting her desktop and tossed them into a trashcan. She flashed Cullen a brave smile. Confused by Ann's concern that the director would see her crying, Shea returned to her chair.

"What's going on?" Cullen asked, shaking Jansen's hand. "Has the museum been robbed?"

Shea guessed the coroner must have already removed Ethan's body.

"No, sir," Jansen replied in a respectful tone. "A murder. A Mr. Ethan Brumley."

"Ethan? That's terrible. A robbery, do you think?"

"Not a robbery. The victim was wearing a ring. His wallet and credit cards were in his pants pocket. Besides, a spear isn't your average mugger's weapon of choice."

A puzzled frown creased the director's brow. "Spear?"

"The war lance, I think," Shea said.

"War lance!" He shot a questioning glance at Ann. "What was Brumley doing with it outside?"

Ann shook her head.

Jansen eyed Shea, a slight smile on his lips.

For crying out loud, Shea, keep your mouth shut. She'd often found that difficult, especially when her emotions ran rampant over her common sense.

The lieutenant turned to Cullen. "Sir, I have a few questions."

"Of course. Anything to help."

"Where were you last night?"

"Santa Fe. I just got back. Myself and Cheek Larson, an artifact dealer." He looked at his Rolex. "About twenty minutes ago. I was on my way home when I saw the police cars."

Shea noted he still wore the same suit and striped silk tie as yesterday.

Ann opened her mouth, but nothing came out. Cullen had flashed a warning glare. Ann's newly found strength seemed to waver, and she turned away.

"You can check with the Santa Fe Museum of Antiquities if you need confirmation," Cullen said to Jansen.

"I'm sure there won't be a problem, sir."

Did Cullen's position prompt this change in the detective,

or did he show more respect when dealing with a man? Either reason grated on Shea.

"Lieutenant?"

The static-riddled voice startled her.

Ann flinched, too, and struggled to keep her composure. Jansen pulled a walkie-talkie from his belt. "What is it?"

"Uh, Lieutenant?"

Officer O'Reilly's voice transmitted clear this time, but hushed, as if he were whispering.

"There's a bunch of Indians down here."

"What?" Jansen pressed and released the call button a few times. "Speak up. I can't hear you."

"I said," O'Reilly blurted, "we got a bunch of Indians here. And they're armed."

Ten

At Cullen's suggestion, to accommodate the new arrivals, they filed into the conference room next to Ann's office. Ann scurried to clear the table where she'd been sorting papers. Shea hefted the last stack and followed her to the row of bookshelves.

"What's going on?" Shea asked.

Ann shook her head and turned to walk away. Shea caught her by the arm. "Something more than Ethan's death is bothering you."

"Not now," Ann whispered, slipping from her grasp.

An uneasy feeling ate at Shea as they rejoined Cullen and Lieutenant Jansen. Before they could sit down, Officers Wolkalski and O'Reilly entered the room with Cheek Larson and the Indians she'd met the day before. They carried tomahawks, knives, two war lances, and a bow with arrows. The steel handle of a Bowie knife protruded from a leather sheath tucked in Cheek's waistband.

A shiver raised goose bumps along her arms. Cheek had the strength to send the knife into a man's chest. Did he also have a reason?

Jansen stiffened at the sight of the armed men, then rested a fist on his hip, exposing a holstered .38 caliber Smith & Wesson beneath his jacket. The lieutenant's men stood vigilant next to the Indians.

"Lieutenant," Cullen said, "this is artifact dealer Cheek Larson. Behind him are Four Bears, Elk Horn, and Billy Quintella."

The Indians nodded.

Shea, perturbed she cared, wondered why Blade wasn't with them.

"All fine craftsmen," Cullen added, "as you'll note by the artifacts they're returning."

She smiled to herself. The Indians weren't armed. They're returning restored relics. Besides, modern militants would probably tote AK-47s.

"Put them on the table," Jansen said.

Cullen walked to a chair next to Shea and held it out for her. He did the same for Ann.

Jansen remained standing and pointed at the knife in Cheek's waistband. "The machete, too." His other hand hovered close to the Smith & Wesson.

"Bowie knife." Cheek grunted the correction.

"Get rid of it."

Cheek's cold eyes dissected Jansen, as if estimating what sort of opponent the wiry officer would make.

"It's mine."

"On the table." Jansen's tone promised action if Cheek delayed any longer.

Shea didn't envy the lieutenant's position. She wouldn't want to go up against a knife-wielding Cheek Larson, even with a gun and two armed officers nearby.

"Please, gentlemen." Cullen placed a calming hand on Cheek's shoulder. "There seems to be a misunderstanding. Lieutenant, on my instructions, Cheek is acting as a guard for the relics. He dislikes guns and refuses to carry one. I assure you, neither he nor the rest of these men make a habit of brandishing weapons."

Jansen stood his ground, his men alert.

"Cheek," Cullen soothed.

The dealer allowed another second to elapse before he unsheathed the knife. He laid it on the table and sat down.

"And here's Blade Santee," Cullen said for Jansen's benefit. "Head artisan and chieftain of the Dakota Sioux."

A third officer escorted Blade into the room. Shea's breath

caught. The handsome chief nodded at the lieutenant and sat with the other Indians. Although the tension had eased, it would take Cheek's Bowie knife to cut through the animosity.

Keeping his eyes on Jansen, Blade ignored Shea once again.

Her lips pressed into a firm line. What was the old saying? *Fooled once, shame on you. Fooled twice, shame on me.* He'd not get a second chance to make a fool of her.

Jansen broke the fragile silence. "It's getting crowded. You ladies can go for now."

Generally, a standard interrogation was conducted on an individual basis. If Jansen let the others stay, he had something up his proverbial sleeve. Fraud had escalated to murder, and Shea's good name was headed for the dumpster. She wanted to hear what they had to say. Determined, she grasped Ann's arm in protest.

"As curator of this museum, I'm responsible," Ann said with recovered authority. "I have a right to hear what information these men have."

"So you're responsible for Brumley's murder?" Jansen asked.

Ann's eyes widened. Her mouth dropped open, but nothing came out.

"Murder!" Cheek blurted. "What murder?"

Shea glanced at the dealer. Did he think the police were here about a forged artifact?

Realizing how Jansen must see them, Shea surveyed the table full of possible suspects. Except for Billy, who cast a fleeting peek at Blade, the rest of the Indians remained emotionless. Did the young man know something? Was he seeking guidance from his chief? Her focus darted to Jansen, whose eyes rested on Billy. As the questioning got under way, no more mention was made of Shea and Ann leaving.

Cheek's alibi matched Cullen's. "I flew Mr. Gerard to Santa Fe. To check out some pottery. Waste of time."

"Waste of time?" Jansen asked.

Cullen cut in. "The pottery wasn't as old as expected. And in bad shape. Not up to museum standards."

"I'll need a copy of your flight plan."

"Of course. Cheek will get that for you."

"What about you?" Jansen directed the question at Elk Horn.

"We all stayed late at the workshop. To meet Mr. Gerard's deadline."

"All of us," Four Bears cut in. "Including Blade."

"That's your alibi, too?" Jansen said to Blade.

"Yes," Blade responded.

"So you're each other's alibis?"

Blade and his men nodded in unison.

"How convenient. Let me get this straight," Jansen said. "Miss McKenna and Miss Scott are the only ones without alibis?"

No way! Jansen considered her a suspect? Her professional reputation sullied by association, yes, but a suspect?

"And Mr. Gerard and Geronimo, here," he thumbed the inflammatory reference at Cheek, "claim they were 8,000 feet in the air at the time of Brumley's death."

Cheek shifted in his chair and uttered Indian epithets under his breath.

Jansen ignored him and went on. "No offense, Mr. Gerard, but with a private plane landing at a private airfield, you could have returned anytime."

Cheek rose halfway out of his seat and rested his meaty hands on the table. "You're not laying this on us. Mr. Gerard and me was in Santa Fe. Why ain't you shooting holes in *their* alibis?" He motioned toward the other Indians. "Their workshop's in the park. They could've killed Brumley."

Four Bears lumbered to his feet. Blade stood and placed a restraining hand on the big Indian's back.

Jansen smiled. "What about the Chief and his band of merry men?"

Blade glared at Cheek. Anger spread across his face as he spoke in even tones to the dealer.

"*Un wa-sas-ki-ye tu-we nis i-ya-nun-pa.*"

"What's that, Chief?" Jansen asked. "In English."

"Cheek Larson hired us for this job. Now he accuses us of murder?"

The other Indians nodded in support of their chief.

"Please," Cullen said, "Everyone calm down."

Four Bears' gaze switched to Cullen. "This man and Cheek verified the relics."

Ann came to the director's defense. "Cullen's credentials are impeccable. I'm not that familiar with Cheek's background."

Cheek exploded. "What about you? Don't be fooled 'cause she's a woman, Jansen. She's got trophies in her office from when she was a champion javelin thrower. Not much difference between a javelin and a lance."

"That was in my college days. I haven't touched a javelin in years."

Oh, my god. Shea had been there when Ann's coach declared her skill with a javelin Olympic material. Could Ann... Would Ann?

Jansen leaned back in his chair. His lack of socially acceptable dialogue and his willingness to allow them to hear each other's statements had shocked her, until she realized there was cunning in his folly. He was letting them hang themselves. Despite her concern for Ann, she decided to keep her mouth shut—for the moment.

"None of these men know how to throw a lance?" Ann added with a smirk.

"A lance is just as deadly thrown by a woman," Four Bears countered.

Shea found it impossible to remain quiet another second. "This is ridiculous. What reason would Ann have to kill Ethan? She rehired him."

Jansen finally spoke. "I'll answer that for you. Say Mr. Gerard and Cheek verify the artifacts. But before the items are taken to Santee and his men to be restored, Miss Scott switches the relics with fakes."

"I'd recognize a fake," Blade said.

"So either you two are in cahoots, or she switches it after it's restored. Then hires an old man with failing eyesight to catalog the forged artifacts, thinking he won't notice. As an added precaution, she hires Miss McKenna to do the photographing. Sorority sisters, right?"

"What?" Shea couldn't believe the insinuation. Did he think a sorority was some secret society that shields its members from the law? "Ann is the curator of this museum and a respected professional. Why would she risk dealing in stolen artifacts? Why would I, for that matter?"

"Money," Jansen said. "Look, I've got the director of the Gateway to the West Historical Society, the curator of the Missouri Westward Museum, the number one Indian artifact dealer in the United States, and the future chief of the Dakota Sioux as suspects." He grunted a laugh. "You might say, Miss McKenna, I've got too many chiefs and not enough Indians. What it boils down to is somebody at this table killed Brumley."

"You can drop my men and me from your list," Blade said. "We were together at the workshop. We'll swear to it."

Except when they delivered the restored relics to the museum. Surely, Jansen realized that. She thought she saw two dark figures last night just inside the new gallery. Was it Blade and one of his men? Ann and Ethan? Cheek and Cullen? Who was lying?

"You and your men are at the top of my list." Jansen leaned back in his chair again. "One of you could've hidden in the museum in case Brumley found proof of a forgery and gotten rid of him."

Great minds think alike. Shea studied the Indians. Elk Horn seemed so passive when she first met him. Was that an act? Four Bears, blatant in his dislike for her, for Ann, for everything and everyone involved with the museum, restrained his anger earlier. Would he have spared Ethan if they'd met alone in a dark corridor? Billy Quintella's youthful goodwill could be as much a sham as Elk Horn's meekness. And what about Blade?

The chieftain stood with his fists clenched. "If a switch was made, it happened at the museum."

"So you say," Jansen responded.

Resentment darkened Blade's eyes. He leaned over the table and its array of weapons. "Am I under arrest?"

Jansen braced at the sudden move. "No one's under arrest. Yet."

"Then my men and I have nothing more to say until we speak to a lawyer. An Indian lawyer."

"That's your right. Nobody's trying to dump the blame on you Indians."

"Where have I heard that before?" Blade's tone was as icy as Jansen's.

Eleven

The morning's hostile uprising in the museum's conference room made Custer's last stand pale in comparison. Desperately needing to distance themselves from Ethan's death, Shea and Ann retreated to Ann's apartment in the Central West End. The neighborhood east of Forest Park sported a hip and trendy enclave of antique shops, art galleries, bookstores, and sidewalk cafes.

Shea had questions, but her friend's silence signaled she was too upset to discuss the matter. Instead Shea turned in a slow circle in the middle of Ann's living room. "You've redecorated."

Burgundy lamps and chrome and glass end tables flanked an overstuffed white leather couch. A large watercolor of mauve, wine, and white chrysanthemums hung on the wall. Sunlight seeped between slats of Levolor blinds on a window that overlooked the park.

Shea thought of her own renovated carriage house with its eclectic décor. Oriental rugs gleaned from bazaars in Istanbul. China vases bought in out-of-the-way shops in Hong Kong. Grass wall mats from Sri Lanka. She needed some order, if not a road map, in her chaotic life.

"Cullen thought the place stuffy." Ann walked to a bar in a corner of the room. "He suggested the colors and glass tables to give a feeling of space."

Shea nodded. "Very nice."

The director apparently influenced Ann's life more than Shea realized. His furtive glances that muzzled Ann during Jansen's interrogation confirmed it.

"How are your grandmother and aunt?" Ann asked.

"Fine."

Ann had asked the same question at lunch yesterday. She was more rattled than she let on.

"Kathryn's giving a lecture at Cape today," Shea added.

"She's coming to the Ball tonight, isn't she?"

"She'll be there, along with Jonathan Wakefield and Gram. And Philip Ross."

"You still seeing him?"

"No. About Ethan—"

"Do we have to talk about it?" Ann's jagged movements behind the bar escalated.

"I think we need to."

Ann squeezed her eyes shut for a moment.

"I *need* a drink first. Preferably cold and alcoholic." She said the last as if the combination were a magic potion that would make her troubles disappear. "A double. Can I fix you something?"

"Pepsi."

Ann set a bottle of scotch on the counter, then ducked below its granite top.

Smoke-tinted tiles behind the bar reflected Shea in disconnected sections. That's how she felt. Disconnected. First, the forged lance had cast a shadow over her life. Then Blade's strange behavior. Then Ethan's death. Now, doubts about Ann crept into her thoughts. She searched the tiles for a clue to what was happening as if she could fit them together like pieces of a jigsaw puzzle.

Along with glassware, swizzle sticks, and bottles of booze, javelin trophies bearing Ann's name adorned the back bar. Olympic material, that's what their coach had said. Taller and more solidly built than Shea, Ann possessed the physical capabilities to kill Ethan.

The thought horrified Shea. Was Ann involved in a forgery scam? Had she panicked when Ethan came to her office with proof?

Ann rose and placed a napkin and rock glass filled with ice

on the bar. She added a splash of white soda, then poured scotch to the brim. She took a large gulp. Another. Her eyes watered, and Shea wondered if it was from the scotch or Ethan's murder or the trouble she faced.

"Sorry," Ann apologized. "I needed that. I'll get your Pepsi." Her friend seemed to be teetering on an emotional high wire.

"No hurry."

Ann disappeared into the kitchen with a filled glass of scotch. She returned shortly with Shea's soda, her scotch glass empty again.

"Have a seat," Ann said on her way back to the bar. "You're making me nervous standing there."

"Why don't we retrace our steps to see how Ethan missed you last night?" Shea suggested as she sunk into the couch. "Maybe if we talk this out, you'll feel better. I know I will."

Ann sighed in surrender. She made herself another drink and joined Shea. At this rate Ann would be comatose before Shea's questions were answered.

"What time did you leave the museum?"

"Shortly after midnight." Ann's eyes closed in concentration. "I was going through the old catalog sheets. My hands were dusty, so I went to wash them. I came back, locked my office, and left the museum by the back door." Her eyes opened. "Quarter after twelve."

"The janitor was working in the second floor hallway when I went to your office. Did you see him?"

"Joe or his partner Bob?"

Shea remembered the nametag on the man's coveralls. "Joe."

"He was in and out. Emptying trashcans and such. I didn't notice him when I returned from the restroom."

"Okay, let's say Joe goes into your office. Empties the trash. Goes into another room."

"I slip out to wash my hands," Ann offered.

"Ethan leaves the storeroom with the lance and comes to your office. Joe's in the hallway. He sees Ethan."

"Joe assumes I'm there, because the light's still on."

Shea's recitation picked up speed. "He goes down to the supply room in the basement for his mop. Meanwhile, Ethan finds your office empty, waits a few minutes, decides you've gone home, and leaves."

"I come back from the restroom, lock up, and go home."

"I drop by to say good night. Your office is locked and dark. Joe returns from the supply room with the mop." She scowls at Ann. "This whole scenario reminds me of the Keystone Cops. Everyone running in and out of doorways, just missing each other."

"It seems involved, but plausible." A glimmer of hope brightened Ann's words. "Do you think Lieutenant Jansen will see it that way?"

Shea shrugged. "But where did Ethan go after he left your office? He didn't come back to the storeroom. Did he decide to go home, too? If so, why'd he take the lance with him?"

"Maybe he didn't know who to trust and wanted to keep it safe until he talked to me. If the lance is fake, he might've been afraid it would disappear, along with the evidence to support his claim. He wouldn't worry about taking a forgery out of the museum."

"He wanted me to photograph only the items he'd cataloged. Surely, he knew I'd run out of work soon."

Shea thought a moment.

"It's a small thing, but he left without his coat," she added, realizing she'd forgotten to bring it back to the museum.

"Ethan was a fine historian, but everyday things, like remembering his coat or umbrella..." Ann's eyes brimmed with tears. She wiped them with the paper napkin wrapped around her scotch. "If I hadn't brought him back to the museum...now he's dead."

Ann's lips trembled.

Shea felt guilty suspecting her friend and patted Ann's hand. "You can't blame yourself."

Ann's peaches-and-cream complexion turned pallid. Was she in shock over Ethan's death? Understandable. Appalled by the method? Absolutely. Concerned for the museum's reputation under her watch? That's her duty. But something more bothered her. As a friend, Shea felt honor bound to find what it was, to help if she could.

"Ann, I noticed something unspoken passed between you and Cullen during Jansen's interrogation. If you know anything that could clear you, you need to tell the police."

Ann stared into her empty rock glass as if it were a crystal ball that would reveal a satisfactory answer. None forthcoming, she set the glass on the coffee table and leaned against the couch.

"If Jansen discovers Cullen and I are lovers, he might think we're partners in the forgery. And Ethan's murder."

Shea understood her friend's concern, but something still puzzled her. "Why did Cullen hush you when he told Jansen he'd just returned from Santa Fe?"

A distraught look filled Ann's eyes. "Because he hadn't. When I left last night, I ran into Cullen outside. He was on his way home, saw the light in my office, and felt guilty that I was working late. He suggested a nightcap, and we ended up back here."

She hesitated, as if weighing whether she should tell Shea.

"He spent the night," she finally said. "He didn't mention it to Jansen, because he didn't want to embarrass me. Neither of us killed Ethan. We're each other's alibi."

Ann and Cullen lied. But why?

"Ann, that's good for you and Cullen. If Jansen continues to badger you about your javelin-throwing expertise, you have to tell him you two were together when Ethan was murdered."

"Cullen would never let me carry this alone. He's very protective. He wants to know where I am every minute." She got that dreamy look again. "He can't stand to be away from me." She squared her shoulders. "Besides, Monday we'll have the lance re-evaluated. If it's not a forgery, then Jansen's line of questioning will be moot."

Ann picked up her glass, saw it was empty, frowned, but clung to it as if it were a security blanket. "Maybe we'll never know who killed Ethan. St. Louis doesn't rank as the nation's murder capitol for nothing. And the park's not untouched by the statistics. It's hard to believe that back in the '40s, before air conditioning, people—families—brought blankets and pillows and slept on the ground. Now, even with the mounted patrol, we're not immune to muggings, sexual liaisons in the restrooms, and drug deals gone bad." Her voice turned pensive. "Cullen and I could've scared the killer away when we walked to the parking lot."

Ann pressed the napkin to her nose and sniffled.

Regaining her composure, she added, "So many wonderful things were happening in my life. Meeting Cullen. The Guggenheim within reach. My hard work finally showing results. Now—it's so unfair."

It didn't seem fair to Shea either, but then, Ethan's death wasn't fair. She wished she had more answers.

Despite her own turmoil, Shea acquiesced. "You're probably right. This whole thing will be cleared up soon, and everyone associated with the museum will be vindicated."

Vindicated, but not forgiven. She wondered how her own career would fare after the news spread that she'd been involved, even innocently, in fraud and murder. Ann's secret affair with Cullen won't help matters. It disturbed Shea and would surely upset the Historical Society's board of directors. Not to mention the Guggenheim board. There went Ann's appointment.

So, if Ann and Cullen had an alibi, Blade would be next on Jansen's list of suspects. The handsome chieftain's interest in her, then his rejection, left her doubting his veracity. She wished she were on assignment in India photographing a man-eating tiger. There'd be no doubts about the big cat's intentions.

Ann's bedroom phone interrupted Shea's efforts to make sense of what she'd learned.

"That was Cullen," Ann said when she returned. "The police are finished at the museum, and he wants me to complete the cataloging. He'll be busy displaying the artifacts."

She glanced at her watch and snatched up her car keys.

"We've only five hours before the Ball. There's the caterer and chamber music group to set up. Patron's books to be laid out. Last minute details to attend to." She paused and turned to Shea. "I don't mean to sound callous. Circumstances have put us behind schedule. Will you help?"

The desperate look in Ann's eyes told Shea her friend's request involved more than preparing for the Patrons Ball. A plea for acceptance? Confidentiality?

"Of course I'll help."

Shea wondered who would help sort out the mess *her* life had become.

Twelve

Throughout the day, Blade and Cheek, or one of the other Indians, brought more relics from the workshop and deposited them in the museum's storeroom. Cullen commandeered the men to help with the displays. Ann cataloged while Shea photographed. Blade still refused to acknowledge anything had ever transpired between them.

"How many pieces are ready?" Cullen asked Ann.

"You're not making our work easier checking every five minutes," she said.

"Sorry. I'm a little anxious. Let me buy you each a cold drink from the soda machine."

"Pepsi," Shea said.

Ann nodded. "Same for me."

As he turned to leave, Blade and Cheek carried in the buffalo hide shield Shea had seen Four Bears restoring. Wisps of white horsehairs attached with silver and turquoise studs formed a circle in the shield's center. Inside the circle, some long-dead Indian had painted a fading buffalo head.

A smile spread across Cullen's face. "Magnificent. Hurry with that, Shea, I have just the spot for it."

While she snapped shots from different angles, she noticed Blade and Cheek failed to share Cullen's enthusiasm. Was something wrong with the shield, or were the two men still chafing from Lieutenant Jansen's interrogation?

"How many more relics are at the workshop?" Ann asked.

"Elk Horn and Billy are bringing the last few that are to be displayed." Blade turned to Shea. He seemed to want to speak to her.

"Have you catalogued it, Ann?" Cullen asked.

"Yes."

"Great. Blade, would you and Cheek carry the shield to the gallery? I want to make sure this goes on the wall for tonight's gala. It's exquisite."

Shea watched Blade's strong hands lift the weighty relic. Her pulse quickened when she remembered the touch of those hands in the tepee.

His back muscles flexed beneath his flax-colored gauze shirt. A braided forelock laced with a red feather fell across his shoulder. She continued to stare as he maneuvered the shield through the doorway.

Cullen slapped a handful of change on the worktable, startling her. "You don't mind getting your own sodas, do you?"

A yelp edged with pain echoed down the museum corridors. Ann had gone for sodas, but the cry didn't sound like a woman's voice. Shea abandoned her camera and raced toward the new gallery, arriving seconds before Ann. Blade entered next, trailed by his men. Cheek plodded in last.

They gaped at Cullen, who stood on a stool facing the wall, the buffalo shield anchored above his head. An Arikara bone knife pinned his up-stretched arm to the display's backboard. Bright red stained his sleeve.

Ann's scream broke the spell.

"I'm all right." Cullen sounded brave, but in pain. "Give a hand, Cheek, and remove this blasted knife."

Before Shea could warn him not to smear any prints, the dealer pulled the knife free.

Cullen slumped onto the stool.

Ann rushed to his side. "Call an ambulance. Call the police. Get him some help."

"We'll call both," Blade said and headed for the corridor. Billy and Elk Horn followed close on his heels.

Cheek whipped a bandanna from his pocket and tied a tourniquet above Cullen's wound.

"Who did this?" Ann's voice verged on hysteria.

Cullen shook his head. "I don't know. After Cheek and Blade hung the shield and left, I climbed on the stool to straighten it. My back was to the gallery entrance." His face contorted as he gripped his arm. "I didn't see anyone."

Cheek cursed. "First Ethan. Now Mr. Gerard. Next time it might be one of us."

Fear filled Ann's eyes. She pressed closer to Cullen. "Who would do this? Why?"

"Who wasn't here?" Cheek asked.

Everyone paused, then said in unison, "Four Bears."

"Now, wait," Shea said. "Blade and the other Indians were here, so Four Bears is probably standing guard at the workshop."

"Or taking the opportunity to kill Cullen," Ann said. "Or whoever he caught alone."

"I don't think this was an indiscriminate attack," Shea said. "Cullen insisted the lance be rechecked. If it's a forgery, Jansen's investigation would zero in on our little group for sure."

"Four Bears is unhappy we have the relics. He thinks they should be returned to the tribes," Cullen said through teeth clenched in pain. "They don't have the finances to properly care for them, nor display them. For heavens sake, they can't even afford to build a health clinic. That's what this is all about. To protect the relics and raise funds for a hospital on the reservation. Can't he see that?"

Cheek nodded. "He could be planning to kill us all. In retribution."

"I don't believe he's that psychotic—or stupid," Shea said. "With Blade and his other tribesmen here, he'd have no alibi. Besides, someone working at the museum might recognize him."

"We all look alike to you white eyes," Cheek snarled.

Cullen clutched his arm and groaned.

"Hang on," Ann said. "An ambulance should be here soon." Determination replaced the concern in her eyes. "This settles it. I'm canceling the Ball."

Cullen shook his head. "I won't hear of it. It's not serious. Someone just drive me to the hospital."

Before they could respond, sirens wailed in the distance.

"See, the ambulance will be here any second." Ann turned to Shea. "I'm going with Cullen. Could you make sure everything's ready for tonight?"

Cullen managed a brave smile and patted Ann's trembling hand. "You finish preparing for the Ball. I shall attend, no matter what."

"Do you think you should?" Shea asked.

"A bandage and fresh clothes, and I'll be good as new."

"Yes, but someone tried to kill you. Next time, he may not miss."

Cheek clutched the hilt of the Bowie knife tucked in his waistband. "I'll stay close to him."

Shea wondered how adept the dealer was with the hefty knife—or an Arikara bone knife. She looked around for the weapon that nearly cost the director his life and found it atop a glass showcase. She recognized it as one she'd photographed. Her gaze traveled around the room, searching for the spot where the knife had been displayed.

An empty set of clamps hung on the wall at the gallery entrance. A tomahawk, a bow and several flint-tipped arrows, knives from various tribes, and a lance similar to the one that killed Ethan were displayed nearby. Anyone bent on dealing Cullen the same fate had an arsenal from which to choose.

She slipped away for a closer look at the weapons. Something red on the floor caught her attention. More blood? Bending nearer, her heart sank when she saw a red feather, like the one braided in Blade's forelock.

Had he lost it while carrying in the shield or when throwing the bone knife?

"I'll take that." Lieutenant Jansen gave her a hard look as he entered the gallery. "In the future, don't touch anything. You could be destroying evidence."

The cavalry had arrived.

Thirteen

Shea lay across Kathryn's bed among a rainbow of discarded evening gowns her aunt had tossed there. "I need to talk to you."

The sweet scent of summer roses wafted in through the second-story window. She could hear Gram humming a Scottish love song as she worked in the flower garden below. Hardly apropos considering Shea's love life was in the pits.

"Fire away." Her aunt held up a pale blue dress. "What do you think? For the Patrons Ball?"

Shea grimaced.

"Yeah, me too." Kathryn threw it on the bed with the others.

"Kathryn?"

"Go on. Talk. I can listen while I dress." She eyed Shea. "You ready for the Ball?"

Still wearing the jeans and T-shirt she'd donned that morning, Shea rolled her eyes. "Do I look ready for the Ball, Katie?"

"Thought maybe you were making a statement."

"You're starting to sound like Gram."

"God forbid. Shoot me." Kathryn turned and rummaged again in the closet. She generally dressed like her namesake Kathryn Hepburn, slacks and sensible shoes with a silk blouse in the summer or a long-sleeved, turtleneck jersey in the winter. If she was giving a lecture, she threw on a tweed or linen blazer. Seldom-used eveningwear had been relegated to the rear of the closet.

Shea gazed around the room. Her aunt's taste leaned toward the Spartan. Clean, uncluttered, no frills or lace. A black and white color scheme—except for the gowns temporarily thrown on the bed.

That's the way Kathryn conducted her life. Things were either black or white. No frills, devoid of emotional attachments other than family and a handful of friends. If she decided to pick up and head to Africa to dig a well for the Peace Corps or study mating habits of the Kodiak bear in Alaska, she could. No secret that she served as Shea's role model.

But Kathryn would soon turn fifty without a soul mate to share tales of her adventures in her waning years. Her choice, so that was all right. Shea enjoyed the same lifestyle. Footloose and fancy free. For now. But what about later? Was Kathryn the one to advise her? Or would Shea's concerns fall on unsympathetic ears?

Kathryn turned from the search through her closet and narrowed her eyes at Shea. "What's wrong?"

She'd remained quiet too long. "Ethan Brumley's dead."

"Oooh, that's too bad." Kathryn dragged out a yellow chiffon, got a negative shake of the head from Shea, and threw it on the bed. "Who's Ethan Brumley?"

"The museum's registrar. The elderly gentleman I've been working with."

"I'm sorry to hear that. Heart attack?" The next dress to hit the bed displayed puce and chartreuse stripes.

"He was murdered."

Kathryn spun toward Shea. "What?"

"With a Sioux war lance."

"What!"

"Pinned to the ground outside the museum."

Kathryn started to say "what" again but clamped her hand over her mouth. She pushed dresses on the floor and lay on the bed next to Shea. "Start from the beginning."

When Shea finished, they reclined there in silence. Finally, Kathryn said, "That poor man."

"Ethan's dead. Cullen's stabbed. Ann's facing a ruined career. And everyone at the museum involved with the relics are suspects. Including me."

"You? What! You blow into town for a couple of days to kill a total stranger? Then you're off to Mexico? What do they think you are, a globe-trotting assassin?"

"I'm the only one without an alibi for last night. Except for Ann or Cheek Larson, depending on which one is lying about being with Cullen."

"Oh, yeah? Well, every person in St. Louis sleeping single doesn't have an alibi at that time of night."

"Like you?" Darn, she said that out loud.

Kathryn rolled over and peered at Shea. "Something else on your mind?"

"You know that guy I told you about—Blade Santee?"

"Tall, dark, and hunky."

"He's not speaking to me."

"What'd you do?"

Shea bolted upright. Discussing this with Kathryn was a mistake. "What makes you think I did something?"

"You're drop-dead gorgeous with a great figure. You're smart. Exciting. And from the way you talked, you liked him. You must've done something majorly wrong." She said the last like a valley girl and poked dimples into her cheeks.

"Nothing. One minute he's nuzzling my neck. The next, he's acting like I don't exist."

"Have you talked to him about it?"

"I haven't had a chance. There's always someone around."

"Does he know you're working in the museum storeroom?"

"Yeah."

"So if he wants to talk to you, he knows where to find you."

"Do you have to be so pragmatic?"

"In a thirty-six hour period he was interested in you, then he dumped you. Am I right?"

"Yeah."

"What happened in those thirty-six hours that might make him change his mind?"

"I don't know how it matters, but Ethan was murdered."

"So maybe he thinks you killed Ethan."

"Please."

"Just brainstorming possibilities the police will consider."

"Brainstorm in another direction, Hurricane Kathryn."

"Maybe he killed Ethan or knows who did."

"Blade snubbed me before Ethan died, but you could be right. It could somehow be connected. Still, I can't believe he'd kill Ethan."

"That's your heart talking."

"I know, I know. I need to get him to talk to me. Straighten out whatever's the misunderstanding."

"Uh, if he's the murderer, I'd rather you wouldn't."

"Then I have to choose a public place but with no one else too close. So he'll talk, but I'm not in danger. *If* I can get him to talk."

"Is he coming to the Ball tonight?"

"All the Indians are."

"Shouldn't you be referring to them as Native Americans? Maybe that's what ticked him off."

"Not according to Russell Means. Means says the name Indian doesn't come from Columbus supposing he'd found a route to the Indies or to India, labeled Hindustan on his maps. Indian is derived from the Italian phrase 'in dio'—meaning 'in God.' A name Columbus called the tribal people when he washed up on their shores."

"Well aren't you just a little encyclopedia of information. So, Blade's coming to the Ball?"

"Yes."

Kathryn jumped up and rummaged through her closet again. "Good. I've got a little number here that'll make his feathers molt." She whipped out a strapless black satin sheath that could do double duty as a cummerbund.

"Where's the rest of it?"

Kathryn waved the scrap of cloth in front of Shea. The satin swished seductively. "This is it."

It didn't even raise a breeze.

Shea shook her head. "Not on my best day."

"Oh, yeah." Kathryn undulated her hips. "Oh, yeah."

"Never. That wouldn't even make a decent mask for Zorro."

"Oh, yeah."

"No."

"I don't normally advise using sexual wiles to catch a man, but drastic times call for drastic measures."

"No."

"It's never failed me yet."

"You're kidding me. Are you leading a double life? Mild-mannered lecturer in the daytime. Hooker at night. No."

"With your cleavage, he'll be eating out of your hand."

Shea could almost feel Blade licking her palms. A pleasant shiver ran through her. "You got heels to go with that?"

Kathryn threw Shea the dress. "See you at the dance, Nance."

"I'm going out the back, Jack," Shea countered as she sped down the hall.

She felt better already.

Fourteen

The Patrons Ball was in full swing when Shea arrived. Women floated across the museum's marble floor in pastel gowns and slinky dresses. Men sported black ties and dinner jackets or tuxedos. A stringed quartet playing chamber music sat among potted ferns in a corner of the airy glassed-in foyer. Double entry doors opened onto a stone terrace. In its center, a lighted fountain shot streams of water into the night sky.

"Nice," Shea whispered to herself. "Very nice." She'd have to compliment Ann on a job well done.

She checked her reflection to make sure the top of the strapless black sheath Aunt Kathryn had loaned her was still in place. She wanted Blade to notice her, not get herself arrested for indecent exposure.

She glanced around the vestibule for a glimpse of him. Their hot and heavy interlude in the tepee, then his cold attitude in the workshop baffled her. She determined to sort out the real Blade Santee.

Her heart lurched when she saw Lieutenant Jansen and Officers O'Reilly and Wolkalski in tuxedoes surveying the crowd. Clawing at his starched collar and fidgeting with his cummerbund, Jansen stuck out like a preacher in a whore house. She slipped behind a potted plant before he spotted her, but not before Ann did.

"Great. You're here." Ann pulled her from behind the greenery. "Be a pal and help keep everyone entertained until Cullen arrives."

"How's his arm?"

"Bandaged and in a sling. The doctor agreed with Cullen. Just a flesh wound. He's upstairs resting."

Shea squeezed her friend's hand. "Be careful tonight. Lots of people here. I wouldn't want anything to happen to you—to any of us."

Ann flipped open her satin clutch bag. "I want to show you something."

A .25 caliber handgun nestled between a silver compact and tube of lipstick. Ann picked up the pistol with two fingers as if it were a diseased rat.

"For cripe's sake!" Shea shoved the gun back into Ann's purse. "You want every cop in the place to draw down on us?"

"Cullen refuses to stay away from the Ball. I have to protect us. Like you said, there are so many people here."

Ann's voice trailed away as she studied the guests' faces with the same tenacity displayed by Lieutenant Jansen.

"You know how to use that thing?" Shea wasn't a stranger to guns. A collector and career military, Andrew McKenna had made sure his daughter knew how to use one. She'd never aimed a gun at someone, however, much less shoot him. Or her. Could Ann, even in self-defense?

"Cullen loaded it and showed me how to release the safety. All I have to do is aim and shoot. Couldn't be any more difficult than throwing a javelin." Ann grimaced. "Sorry, bad analogy. Cullen's against me carrying a gun," she added. "He hates violence."

Shea spied Jansen near the hors d'oeuvre table. He tugged again at his tuxedo's tight fitting collar and glared at the patrons, daring them to give him a hard time. How would he react to Ann's carrying a gun?

"Then Cullen will be down soon?" Shea asked.

"He likes to wait until most of the guests arrive before he, uh—"

"Makes an entrance?"

"That sounds so orchestrated, I know, but Cullen says every little detail matters when asking people to donate money."

Security settled, Ann snapped shut her loaded purse.

"He's very good at fund-raising. And there's just never enough money for acquiring artifacts. Or quality restoration. Or proper displaying. Or authenticity checks. The list goes on and on."

It sounded contrived to Shea. Everything Cullen did seemed contrived.

This from a woman wearing a doily to attract a man.

She jerked on her dress top. And not just any man but a Sioux Indian chief who'd proven untrustworthy. They'd be committing her to an institution soon.

Ann frowned. "Speaking of orchestrated, why aren't the musicians playing? Mingle while I see what's wrong."

Ann hurried away before Shea could ask her exactly how she should entertain over two hundred guests. Never good at idle chit-chat, she cringed at the thought. Belly dancing, one of the cultural talents she'd picked up in Baghdad while photographing the ruins of an ancient ziggurat, was out of the question. She had no memorized jokes to tell. No impressions to perform. No card tricks up her sleeve. In fact, no sleeves. She tugged again at the top of her gown.

Resigned to her fate, she scanned the elegantly-dressed crowd that represented St. Louis' elite for a familiar face. Descendants of the city's founding families—Chouteau, Laclede, Gratiot—clustered in small groups with bankers, lawyers, doctors, and stockbrokers. Beer barons mingled with sports celebrities. She spotted Jansen huddled with members of the St. Louis Cardinals baseball team and wondered how efficiently he could guard Cullen if he was busy arguing double play strategy.

Unless she could offer an inside tip on some hot stock, the snow cover in Vail, or the best restaurant in St. Moritz, she had little to say that would interest these people. Even though they were here to donate money to the museum, she doubted if they could tell a Neolithic shrimp fossil from a fresh one dipped in cocktail sauce.

Where were Gram and Aunt Kathryn? And Blade?

Not a moment too soon, she spied a bar in the corner. "Pepsi on the rocks," she ordered as she sidled up to a bartender. Caffeine was the monkey on her back, not booze.

"Having a nice night?" he asked. His languid gaze strayed from her face to her cleavage and settled for a long stay.

"Peachy." She tugged at her bodice, downed her drink, and sought a safer spot to wait for Blade.

She noticed the patron's books had been handed out to whet the guests' appetites for what lay beyond the gallery's entrance. Appreciative sounds hummed through the crowd as they reviewed her work. Looking for an opportunity to hand out her business cards, she strolled among them and listened to their comments. In a few moments, they'd witness the real artifacts, and their attention would shift to the talents of Blade and his artisans.

Where were the Indians hiding?

As if summoned by her musings, Four Bears, Elk Horn, and Billy Quintella marched through the vestibule doors. Decked out in brightly colored shirts, buckskin pants, and moccasins, they struck an impressive pose. Hawk feathers hung from beaded headbands. All wore sheathed knives or tomahawks strapped to their thighs, and Billy had slung a bow with quiver and arrows across his back.

Still no Blade.

For the first time, Shea noticed a red and white bullseye balanced against bales of hay at the back of the foyer. A display of Indian prowess evidently headed Cullen's list of ways to part patrons from their money. Oohs and ahs surged through the crowd, punctuated here and there with a nervous giggle. Ann herded the Indians into the throng of admirers.

Four Bears hung back. Either he felt being paraded around like a pet Pomeranian was degrading, or he was shy. Maybe he still harbored the nasty mood he displayed yesterday in the workshop. Had he heard that people suspected him of attacking Cullen? His erect posture with arms folded and frown still in place suggested the latter.

Instead of asking about life on a reservation, the patrons bombarded the Indians with questions about oil wells and casinos. Shea decided to join Four Bears.

"Hello."

"Umph." His black eyes shone with contempt.

"I'm sorry if all this offends you. I believe Cullen's trying to do his best for the new gallery. He seems to be impressed with the work you've done."

The light in Four Bears' eyes flared. "Indian relics belong to the Indian."

"You're probably right."

Uneasy about her own role in the project, she wondered how to show respect for the Indian and still be sympathetic to the work the museum did in preserving the relics. Her friend was the museum curator. And Shea would earn a tidy sum photographing the artifacts.

"Some good comes from the exhibit," she said. "It brings a better understanding of a people greatly wronged and misunderstood. And your work earns money for the much-needed medical clinic."

She admired the proud and talented Four Bears, but just how possessive did he and the rest of the Dakotas feel about the relics? Enough to kill for?

"Where's your chief?"

"Shea, dear."

She turned to see Gram, Aunt Kathryn, and Professor Jonathan Wakefield walking toward her. Gram wore her favorite lace-over-beige-crepe dress and trademark strand of pearls. Wakefield's assistant Philip Ross tagged along behind.

Shea smiled and kissed her grandmother's powdered cheek. "You look lovely." Gram smelled of gardenias and lavender soap.

"Thank you, dear. So do you." She paused, scrutinizing Shea. "Too bad there isn't more of your frock to admire."

Shea rushed on, "I want you all to meet…" When she turned

back to Four Bears, he had disappeared. Perplexed, she aimed Gram's attention toward her aunt.

"Well, I especially like your dress, Kathryn. Isn't that mine?"

"This old thing?" Kathryn smoothed the teal blue floor-length cocktail dress with the hand that wasn't holding Jonathan's.

"Don't paw the professor, Katie." Shea looped her arm through his free one. They'd become good friends in the year and a half since he and Kathryn started dating. "How are you, Jonathan?"

"Fine, thank you. How was Hong Kong?"

Shea's last assignment had her bobbing leisurely for three weeks in a Chinese junket while she shot slides of the Bay of Hong Kong and Victoria Harbour.

"Oriental, Prof. Very oriental. And how are things in the history department?"

"Historical."

"Historical and handsome," she amended as she patted his tuxedo lapels.

A broad smile spread across Jonathan's bulldog face. Shea guessed most of his accolades sprang from his academic accomplishments. To Kathryn's feminist mortification, Shea always made a point of flirting shamelessly with him. It brought out his playful side few people saw, and she could tell he adored it.

"She's leading you down the garden path, Jonathan," Kathryn said.

"And an enjoyable trip it is," he replied and gave Shea a half bow.

Kathryn kissed him on the cheek. "Come on. Let's dance before you make a fool of yourself."

She pulled him out onto the stone terrace filled with couples waltzing to the lilting strains of Franz Schubert.

Gram turned to Philip. "Why don't you dance with Shea?"

"Hello, Philip." Shea smiled warmly, but quickly added, "Philip might not want to dance."

Gram had shifted into her matchmaking mode. Shea searched

her brain for a way to sidestep Gram's endeavors without hurting Philip's feelings. He was a nice guy. She just wasn't interested. She didn't want to lead him on by dancing with him.

"I'd love to dance." Philip held out his hand.

Not unattractive, his slicked-back blond hair reminded her of a 1920s style reminiscent of F. Scott Fitzgerald. He had a nice smile. And his brown eyes glowed enthusiastically as he gazed at her through wire-rimmed glasses.

But they weren't Blade's eyes.

"Then so would I." What else could she say?

Fifteen

"You look beautiful," Philip said as they strolled onto the terrace.

Self-consciously, Shea smoothed her auburn hair. "Thank you."

He took her in his arms and they began to waltz. No sparks flew when they touched. No tingly prickles along her spine. No heavy breathing—at least not on her part.

She noticed Philip's shoulders weren't as broad as Blade's. Although he had a trim physique, neither his stature nor his presence was as impressive as the Dakota chieftain's. Would she be doomed forever to compare suitors—probably absolutely wonderful men—to Blade? She didn't see how she could avoid the dilemma.

"Did your aunt tell you I called?"

Rats!

"Why yes, she did. I've been so busy though, photographing the relics, I haven't had time for a social life."

He smiled. "Oh, I wasn't calling to ask you out. I was curious about your trip before Hong Kong. Jerusalem. Middle East culture's my bailiwick."

Touché. She'd been put in her place—and well deserved. Maybe it was Gram alone who fantasized about a match between them and not Philip. Maybe she should just lighten up and enjoy herself. She returned his smile and his expanded, reaching his eyes.

"Jerusalem was wonderful," she said. "The city glows like gold.

Three of the major world religions—Judaism, Christianity, and Islam—are centered there. But I guess you already know that," she added, remembering Ann's comment about the Pike to her.

"I've been there a few times. As a Christian, certain areas are especially poignant. The Holy Sepulcher. The Mount of Olives. The Dome of the Rock built over Mount Moriah where Abraham planned to offer his son Isaac as a sacrifice."

"Yes, there were moments when no tourists were around, I felt as if I had traveled in time. That when I stood on the Via Delarosa, I was standing exactly where Jesus stood. Touching the things he touched. A moving experience."

Maybe she and Philip did have something in common.

"Anything happening career-wise?" she asked, truly interested.

"Professor Wakefield's planning a trip next month to Mexico. I'm going with him. We'll be doing research on Mayan ruins."

"Really?" Her voice registered her surprise. "I'm headed for the Yucatan Peninsula to do a spread on Mayan ruins next week."

He smiled again. "Next week *is* next month."

"Why, yes, I guess you're right. They've found a temple in what's left of the last rainforest in Mexico. Down near the Guatemalan border."

"Now that *is* a coincidence. The archeological powers-that-be have asked Wakefield to join them in exploring those very same ruins."

She raised a brow. "Imagine that."

Jonathan was an authority on Aztec and Mayan culture. He'd been to Mexico before on similar expeditions. Could Philip have gotten her itinerary from Kathryn? Sure, then went out and trumped up a Mayan temple to further his pursuit of her.

Gee, Shea, your suspicious nature is working overtime. Not to mention your ego.

Ethan's death and all the intrigue it brought had crippled her common sense.

"If it's the same ruin," Philip said. "Maybe we'll see each other."

"Cocktails in Cancun then?"

"It's a date."

They laughed together. She was joking. Somehow, she didn't think he was.

The band dropped their three-quarter waltz beat and switched to the first few bars of "Pomp and Circumstance." Dancing ceased and Shea and Philip returned to the vestibule. All heads twisted toward the museum's winding staircase.

Cullen Gerard strolled down the steps like a posturing peacock, as if he expected trumpets to blare and virgins to cast rose petals in his path. Dressed in a snappy white tie and tuxedo, his elegantly-styled red hair shone in the light of the foyer's crystal chandelier. A white satin sling nestled his wounded arm against his chest.

Before he could speak and capitalize on the moment, however, the foyer doors swung open. Blade Santee strode in, black hair flowing across his broad tuxedoed shoulders. An elaborate Sioux war bonnet sat atop his head, its eagle feathers and beaded leather straps cascading down his back. All eyes turned to the handsome Dakota chieftain.

Men gasped and women fainted. Well, not exactly. But an eager, appreciative stir worked through the crowd. The excitement energized Shea. So did the sight of Blade Santee.

When she dragged her gaze back to Cullen, she was amused to see his radiant smile had slipped into a sulking glare.

Sixteen

Shea watched in amusement as Cullen, with arched brow and somber countenance, descended the marble staircase. From her vantage point on the small rise of steps that led to the new gallery, she could see both Cullen and Blade as the director pushed his way across the vestibule floor to the band. He tapped on the microphone and cleared his throat. "May I have your attention, please?"

All eyes shifted toward him. He adjusted his wounded arm and its white satin sling. A murmur radiated through the crowd. He tried to raise the microphone but, one-handed, managed only to struggle with it. A band member came to his rescue. The musician's kindness and Cullen's obvious bravery in the face of adversity brought a round of applause from the audience.

Cullen's smile returned.

Shea rolled her eyes. This would be a long night.

"I hope you're enjoying the music and hors d'oeuvres," Cullen said to the people. "It's through your generosity that the relics pictured in this year's patron's books will be saved for posterity. It is you who deserve the applause." He clapped by beating his chest above his heart with his good hand.

The throng cheered.

Ka-ching.

"And to show their appreciation for the money you've donated for a clinic to be built on a Dakota reservation, Chieftain Blade Santee and his men will demonstrate with reproductions the efficiency of nineteenth century weapons."

An excited whispering flowed in waves across the room. Shea climbed higher on the steps to the west wing to get an unobstructed view of the Indians. Philip followed her.

Billy Quintella marched fifty paces from the red and white target, turned and drew an arrow from the quiver slung across his back. He balanced the feathered shaft against the five-foot longbow, pulled back the tightly strung horsehair to his cheek, sighted down the arrow, and let go. The shaft's feathers made a ruffling sound as they cut through the tension. A heartbeat later, the flint arrowhead thudded into the bullseye.

Cheers erupted. Blade grinned proudly at Billy.

Next, Cullen introduced Four Bears, who was armed with a tomahawk. The director explained the weapon's many uses other than parting an enemy from his scalp, a heinous act also practiced by the white man to collect bounties on Indians. With amazing skill and little effort, Four Bears buried the tomahawk's sharply-honed blade in a log leaning against the hay bales.

Billy and Elk Horn juggled knives, then took turns playing target while the other deftly severed feathers held against a board. Cheek Larson joined them. They pushed aside potted ficus trees and rolled out a giant sideshow wheel. Cheek tied Billy to the apparatus, spun it, and demonstrated his expertise with knives. Not until Blade stepped forward with a war lance similar to the one used to kill Ethan did the enthralled patrons hush their cheers.

Shea noticed Jansen worming his way to the front of the crowd.

Blade shed his tuxedo jacket and rolled up the sleeves of his tailored white shirt. The muscles along his tan arms flexed as he hefted the lance. Women in the crowd let out a collective sigh. Thunder rolled. Lightning flashed. Shea found it hard to breathe.

Hormones, just hormones.

The handsome chieftain scanned the crowd. His gaze caught hers, then moved slightly to her right where Philip stood, his shoulder touching Shea's. Blade's countenance clouded over. He turned back to the target and balanced one foot in front of the other. Stretching out his left arm as if reaching for the throat of an adversary, his right hand raised the war lance level with his eyes. Locked on target, he stepped forward and let loose the weapon. It sped along an invisible path toward the bullseye. Deftly displacing Billy's arrow, the lance furrowed a tunnel through the hay bale.

The audience exploded with applause. Jansen cast a suspicious eye at Blade, who returned the lieutenant's calculating stare with one equally intense.

"The show's over," the chieftain said.

"And now," Cullen announced, recovering the moment, "what you've all been waiting for."

The band struck a few resonant chords. The director tugged on a tasseled satin pull, and the draperies covering the new gallery's entrance fell away.

"Shall we go in?" Philip offered his arm.

She patted his chest. "There's someone I must talk to. You go ahead."

He paused, his eyes searching hers. Nodding, he walked toward the gallery.

She waited until he was out of sight, then tried to work her way toward Blade. But the crowd surged in the opposite direction, carrying her into the path of Lieutenant Jansen.

"Evening, Miss McKenna."

"Good evening, Lieutenant." She fanned one hand nervously across her bare cleavage.

He nodded over his shoulder toward the bullseye. "Amazing skills the Indians have."

The last thing she wanted to do was talk to Jansen. She and Ann were still suspects, and she didn't want to inadvertently say something that might raise new suspicions in the mind of the police.

"Amazing how Santee drove that lance right through a bale of hay," he said. "Wouldn't take much more to drive it through a man."

Fear for Blade made it difficult to answer. "I-I have no idea."

Jansen stroked his chin. "Wonder if a woman would be able to do that?"

Her thoughts floundered. "Lieutenant, I—"

"Oh, not you, Miss McKenna. No, no." He motioned at her slim biceps and chuckled. "No, not you. I was thinking of Miss Scott. Now there's a healthy girl."

Shea had to admit, Jansen was right. Ann took after her mother's side of the family, who bore the muscular physique of their Welsh and Scottish ancestry.

"Ann has an alibi."

Jansen raised a Dukakis brow. "Is that right?"

Rats! Would she never learn to keep her mouth shut? She vowed to take a course in tight-lipness.

"She was with Cullen last night."

"With Cullen Gerard?" He shot her a look of disbelief. "Then why didn't they tell me that when I questioned them?"

Oh, well, in for a penny, in for a pound.

"They'd been together all night. At Ann's apartment. Cullen didn't want to say that in front of everyone and embarrass her."

"Mister Gerard, he's a gentleman all right."

"I suppose."

"All night, you say?"

Ann was going to kill her, but it was for her friend's own good.

"Yes. Cullen and Cheek returned from Santa Fe earlier than expected. Cullen saw lights in Ann's office, so he stopped to take her to a late dinner. They ended up at Ann's apartment."

"How do you know this?"

"She told me."

"And she told you to tell me?" Jansen asked, clearly surprised.

A hot blush washed over Shea. "Actually, she asked me to keep it a secret." She explained about Cullen's promise to put in a good word for Ann at the Guggenheim, and their fear that any hint of a personal relationship might tarnish the recommendation.

Jansen grinned. "Not very good at keeping secrets, are you?"

Shea's blush reached her toes. She looked around to see if anyone else noticed, but everyone had gone into the gallery.

"No, not very good at keeping secrets at all," Jansen said. "But, *I'm* going to tell *you* a little secret." He spoke out of the corner of his mouth as if he were some sleazy informant, which was how she felt. "I don't think Miss Scott killed Brumley, either. See, I think it was Santee or Four Bears or Cheek Larson. One of the Indians. All big guys with lots of muscle. Now you tell me Gerard was with Miss Scott, which gives them both, or neither, an alibi. And shoots Larson's full of holes. Don't you think?"

She wasn't about to open her mouth again and stick her other foot in. It was getting crowded in there.

Jansen waggled his bushy brows at her. "No opinion? I'll ask Larson. If I were you, I'd watch my back. And I wouldn't trust the other Indians either."

He glanced around as if one might be sneaking up on them. "Even if Larson killed Brumley, he didn't forge any artifacts. From what I've learned, he hasn't got the talent. So there's a partner. And that would be one of the Dakota artists. My money's on Four Bears or Santee."

She could restrain herself no longer. "Why are you telling me all this?"

"Because I think you're an innocent bystander, Miss McKenna. Just like Brumley. I don't want to find any more innocent bystanders with lances run through them or knives in their arms."

"I appreciate your concern, but I have no intention of getting any closer to the Dakotas than a working relationship."

Okay, that was a lie.

"I think Santee has other ideas, the way he looks at you."

Her heart did a back flip.

Jansen's expression grew serious. "Take my advice. Larson and one of those Indians are up to their feathers in this. Watch out."

Officer Wolkalski approached them. Stretching his neck from side to side, he seemed as uncomfortable in formal attire as Jansen. "Lieutenant, the men are waiting for your instructions in the gallery. Lots of people are wandering around. O'Reilly's afraid they're gonna touch something."

"They wouldn't touch the exhibits," Shea said.

"As long as they aren't touching Gerard or Miss Scott, I don't care. That's who we're here to protect," Jansen said to the sergeant. "The relics are museum security's problem."

He glanced back at Shea as if silently trying to convey the danger she was in.

Despite the summer heat, a chill ran through her.

Seventeen

Jansen's dire words had set Shea's nerves on edge. She'd seen Four Bears, Elk Horn, and Billy follow the patrons into the new gallery.

Where was Cheek?

He'd promised to stay close to Cullen, to protect him. She wasn't sure now whether he or any of the Indians could be trusted. The lieutenant didn't seem to think so.

She relaxed when she remembered Ann. The pistol-packing curator had promised to "stand by her man."

The band segued into another waltz. She spied Blade walking toward her, his gait strong and assured. With the war bonnet gone, his long hair spilled across his shoulders and down his form-fitting white shirt. His sleeves rolled down, silver cufflinks glimmered at his wrists. Her heart fluttered. Whether she was responding to the sight of him or the unease at confronting him, she wasn't sure.

"May I have this dance?" he said.

His scent of a woodland glen wove its magic. She could think of nothing she wanted more than to have his arms around her, but Jansen's warning buzzed in her ears like a bad-tempered hornet. Blade's strange behavior at his workshop compounded her worries.

"Aren't you going into the gallery?" she asked.

"I've seen it all."

"I guess you have."

The lieutenant's words faded in the light of Blade's warm

smile. Her thoughts winged their way back to the workshop. This could not be the same man who ignored her in front of everyone. Embarrassed her. Broke her heart. Jansen's words rushed back.

Stay away from the Indians.

Blade took her hand and led her onto the flagstone terrace. Sweeping her into his arms, he pulled her close. A delightful shiver tripped along her spine. Her heartbeat shifted to double time.

Stay away from the Indians.

For a brief moment he held her still. Stars glittered overhead. Strains of a Viennese waltz filled the night. Then he danced her across the terrace, gliding in graceful circles around the lighted fountain.

"Who was that man with you?" he asked.

"What? Who? Oh, yes, that was Philip Ross. He came with my aunt and grandmother and his boss, Professor Jonathan Wakefield. They're all in the gallery. My aunt dates Jonathan."

She rattled on. Had she noted a hint of jealousy in Blade's question?

"Quite an impressive display of marksmanship," she said, regaining her composure and changing the subject.

"Were *you* impressed?" His infectious grin brightened and sent her pulse racing.

"I'm impressed with your physical skills as well as your artistic talent. And it seems you're a good dancer, too."

He spun her around and around until they were breathless from laughing. His strong back muscles rippled beneath her hand as she clung to him. How could she suspect someone with such warmth of murder? All her doubts and fears fled. She was heady with his power, with the warm summer air and starry skies, with the melodious music and bubbling fountain, and with the growing knowledge that she'd be happy having his arms around her for a long, long time.

"If you really want to see good dancing," he said as they slowed to a sensible gait, "come to the powwow tomorrow night."

"Powwow?"

"Here in the park. Next to the woods." He nodded toward a stretch of forest behind the museum.

Vaguely, she saw campers and RVs ringed in a circle in the distance.

"Many tribes will attend. My men and I represent the Dakota Sioux. Would you like to come?"

His eagerness electrified her. "I'd love to. What time?"

"The ceremony starts at sundown. Where do you live?"

"In a carriage apartment behind one of the old houses at Aberdeen Place. Across Skinker." She pointed past the museum, beyond the forest, to the line of majestic homes built at the turn of the 20th century. The house originally belonged to Shea's prosperous Scottish ancestor.

"Come when you hear the drums."

"I'll be there."

It would give her a chance to learn additional information regarding the Dakotas—and Blade.

"Tell me more about yourself," he said, as if reading her mind. "I know you're an excellent photographer. I've seen the patron's books."

"Thank you. There's not much to tell. I come from strong pioneer stock—"

The words were spoken before she realized what the coming of the settlers meant to his people.

"Ah, yes. The pioneers," he said with mock seriousness in a gracious effort to put her at ease.

"Sorry."

Funny how things looked different standing in someone else's moccasins. Still, if they were to have a healthy relationship, she couldn't forever be apologizing for her ancestors.

"Not your fault," he said. "Go on."

"I chose photography as a career because I wanted to capture the ever-changing world in pictures. To bring my own interpretation to what I saw. Some fascinating people and places and wildlife are being lost forever to encroaching civilizations.

I guess I do with my camera what you do with a paint brush."

"Then we're a lot alike in our goals."

A warm, harmonious sensation filled her. "Yes, I guess we are."

"You say your family's here. I'd like to meet them."

"As soon as they return from the gallery."

Kathryn would love Blade. Gram would too, even though she feared he'd whisk her away to a reservation. Jonathan, ever the professor, would drill him with anthropological questions. And Philip—Shea really didn't know how Philip would respond to another man encroaching on his hunting grounds.

"Is there a Mister McKenna that shares your dreams?" Blade asked.

Nothing like being straightforward. He'd asked about a boyfriend yesterday, now a husband. Was that an Indian trait, that bold frankness? She liked it.

"Yes," she answered.

Blade's smile twisted into a frown.

"But he's retired from the military and lives in Washington, D. C. Works for the government. I guess that's where I get my wanderlust. Moving from base to base in my youth."

"Ah, then you've lived on a reservation, too. Sort of."

Shea marveled at the analogy. She'd never thought of herself as being confined, restricted. But at bases in Muslim countries like Saudi Arabia, women couldn't drive a car or leave the compound unescorted by a man.

"In my teens," she confessed, "I rebelled at leaving behind friends to move to the next military base. I stayed out late. Smoked a little pot. My father sent me to live with his mother and sister here in St. Louis."

"Ah, so you've smoked a peace pipe, too."

"There's pot in those?"

He grinned and shook his head.

"Do you want to hear this or not?"

"Please, go on."

"I don't know why my father thought sending me to live with

Kathryn and Gram would curtail me."

"Didn't your mother object to his sending you away?"

"My mother died when I was fourteen. Car wreck. That was part of the problem. He just couldn't handle me alone."

"So we have something else in common. We both have lost our mothers. Mine to cancer. Two years ago."

"I'm so sorry." She looked away, her eyes misting over their loss. She often grieved for her mother. She would've liked to have known her as an adult.

"Have you ever been to South Dakota?" he asked, drawing her back to him.

She smiled and, regaining her composure, answered in a cheery voice. "No. Is someone keeping the home fires burning for you?"

After all, he just invited her to a powwow. She needed to know his status.

"My father is chief. I have three younger brothers. My mother's death...I admit I have a personal reason for wanting a clinic built on the reservation. Not that it would have saved her, but her last days might have been less painful with the proper care."

"Couldn't she have gone away to a hospital?"

"She wouldn't do for herself what others of the tribe couldn't afford to do, even if she was a chief's wife."

Shea heard the Indian woman's pride in her son's voice. "I'm sorry," she said, once again.

Her pity seemed to unsettle him. Something hard glinted in his eyes. "Our ancestors cannot rest in peace while their bones and possessions are displayed in museums. They need a proper Indian burial." He shook his head. "But, I must weigh the need for a clinic. The closest one is sixty miles away. Our young and our sick die needlessly."

"I'm sorry. Again."

"And again, it's not your fault."

"I may not have caused the problem," she said with conviction. "But we've all added to the injustice by not speaking out. The plight of the American Indian has been ignored too long. I suppose it's because we don't want to be reminded of our mistakes."

He nuzzled her ear and whispered, "We may have to make an honorary Indian out of you at the powwow tomorrow night."

She tried not to notice the goose bumps he'd raised along her arms. "I guess I do have a tendency to get on my soap box."

"Nothing wrong with that." He looked deep into her eyes. "We're a proud people. Not looking for handouts. Just fairness and an opportunity to better ourselves."

"Now that you've stirred my—indignation, I can hardly wait for the powwow."

He held her closer, touching his cheek to hers.

"Blade, about yesterday. In the workshop." God, she didn't want to do this, but she needed to address the 800 pound gorilla waltzing along with them. "Why did you ignore me?"

He drew in a breath, then exhaled deeply. "I'm sorry. I had a lot on my mind. Cullen's deadline. Preparing for our display of weaponry skills tonight. And I'd just received word from my father that Wild Horse, my youngest brother, has been involved in trouble off the reservation."

Shea silently chastised herself. His reasons were valid and important. She felt like a whiny child. "Is your brother all right? The trouble's not too bad, I hope."

"Let's just say he comes by his name naturally. Dad wants me to talk to him."

"So you'll be leaving soon?"

"Besides needing to talk to Wild Horse, my work here is finished. I must return to my people and make plans for the clinic. If more money is needed, I have to find other ways to get funding. Travel and paint more pictures. Restore more relics. I live a nomad's life, like when my people followed the buffalo. Only I follow the elusive dollar."

"I see." And she'd wasted what little time they had pouting. She hadn't thought about his leaving, but of course he must. The clinic. His work. He was as much a professional gypsy as she.

"That is, when Lieutenant Jansen's finished with me."

Reality flooded in, drowning her once again in the starkness of Ethan's death. Here she was enjoying herself while the poor man wasn't even buried yet, and his murderer still on the loose. The stars didn't seem as bright anymore.

"Has the lieutenant learned anything new about Ethan's murder?" she asked. If he had, he didn't mention it to her. Did Blade see her talking to Jansen?

"He ordered the lance re-evaluated tomorrow, instead of Monday." Blade's voice sounded resigned, as if he already knew what the experts would find.

The thought chilled her. *Did* he know the lance was a forgery? If so, she was dancing in the arms of a murderer—or his accomplice. She pulled away. The playful flirtation between them vanished.

"What will the lieutenant find?" she asked.

She had to know the truth, no matter if it broke her heart. Had Blade done what he thought best for his people, even if it meant murder? His mother died a painful death for lack of medical treatment. Might he not see any action to bring a clinic to the reservation a justifiable means to a necessary end?

"Don't let this come between us," he said.

"What will Jansen find?"

A muscle twitched along his jaw line. He closed his eyes for a moment, then opened them and looked into hers. But he remained quiet.

Words of reproach welled inside her. She wanted him to tell her he was innocent. That he had nothing to do with Ethan's death or the forged war lance so they could put this behind them. Get on with their lives. But his silence condemned him as lethally as a confession.

"I see," she whispered.

Turning, she walked away, her heart as cold and unyielding as the terrace stones beneath her feet.

Eighteen

Somewhere on the other side of Shea's closed eyelids, birds sang. She couldn't imagine why. She'd spent the night tossing and turning and running from Indians on the warpath until she fell exhausted into a deep sleep.

So why were the birds so darn happy?

The sun must be shining.

She shot out of bed and cast a frantic glance at the clock on her nightstand. Red digital numbers flashed 11 a.m. Although the deadline for finishing the patron's books for the Ball had passed, she still needed to complete the catalog shots. In one more day she'd be leaving on her next assignment. And Blade would be going back to the reservation.

Thoughts of the Ball brought bittersweet memories. The feel of his arms around her conflicted with the sight of him plunging a lance into a hay bale, the way he could've plunged it into Ethan's body. His warm breath against her cheek while they danced warred with the knowledge that with that same breath he could be lying about his part in fraud and murder.

She wanted to believe in him, but his refusal to answer her questions disturbed her. Why didn't he simply lie? Would a lie be so difficult for a thief and murderer? But if he's innocent, why doesn't he say so. And if so, who *is* to blame? Her friend Ann? A depressing thought. Still, someone involved with the relics was the only logical connection.

She pondered the possibilities as she showered and dressed.

Cullen? He'd been in Santa Fe with Cheek when Ethan died, or in bed with Ann, depending on who lied. Besides, someone attacked Cullen, too.

Cheek had no alibi, but Lieutenant Jansen thought he lacked the expertise to create the lance, so who was his artistic cohort?

One of the Indian craftsmen. She crossed Billy Quintella off her list. He looked too young to be guilty of anything more sinister than a bad case of zits. That left Four Bears and Elk Horn.

Only one way to find the guilty parties. She'd do a little investigating herself, for her own peace of mind, if nothing else. To clear Ann's name. And hopefully Blade's. And for Ethan.

At noon, she burst into Ann's office with a deluge of questions, but Ann wasn't there. Invoices, contracts, and spreadsheets lay strewn across her desk. Glancing around to make sure she was alone, Shea fingered the papers. For a brief second, she experienced a twinge of guilt. What would Ann think if she found her best friend rifling through museum documents?

Won't be any worse than when she finds out you spilled your guts to Jansen about her and Cullen.

Shea gritted her teeth.

I did this for Ann's own good. The truth shall set you free.

Unfortunately, it could also get you arrested.

A quick survey of the desktop turned up an expense sheet listing various services and supplies for the Ball. She let out a low whistle at the bottom line.

"Impressive."

These soirees must bring in enough donations to warrant the cost. And half of the proceeds would go to the medical clinic.

She fumbled through more papers but couldn't find any figures on donations. She searched the desk drawers. Her insides churned for encroaching on Ann's privacy. Were her actions disloyal? The manila folder she found in a bottom drawer eased that guilt. Bold black letters labeled the file: SIOUX WAR LANCE.

A color photograph of the lance popped out at her. She flipped it over and found a name, phone number, and an address in an obscure little town in New Mexico penciled on the back. She wondered if that's who owned the lance. Ethan said Cheek often ferreted out relics in dusty attics.

Pausing, she listened for footsteps on the hall's marble floor. Hearing none, she reached for Ann's phone and dialed the number. Someone picked up on the sixth ring.

"Hello." The wizened voice sounded as old as the lance.

"Hello. Is this—" Shea read the name on the back of the photo, "—Tillie Carwile?"

"Yes."

"This is Shea McKenna at the Missouri Westward Museum. You sold a Sioux war lance to us?"

Suspicion crept into the woman's voice. "Don't want the fifty bucks back, do ya?"

Fifty bucks!

"No, no. We're just checking on the lance's background. How did you acquire it?"

"Acquired it when I acquired my third husband, rest his soul." The woman added the last in a reverent tone. "Said he got it from his great-grandpa who fought the Indians. After the mister passed away, I didn't want that old junk lying around. Means nothing to me. Mr. Larson paid me a good price for the whole works."

"There are more items?"

The woman rattled off a short list of artifacts. "Powder horn, knife, and a quiver with no arrows. Hawk painted on the quiver. Husband said the Indians believed the hawk's spirit made the arrows fly straight."

Shea had photographed the quiver.

"How much did Mr. Larson pay you for all that?"

"Two hundred and fifty bucks," the woman said as if she'd made the deal of the century. "Just old Indian junk, cluttering up the house."

"Thank you. And don't worry. No one wants the money back."

Not at those prices.

Shea wondered how many widows and orphans Cheek stole

from and understood Ethan's distaste for the dealer. Of course, Cheek was no different from any other businessman trying to make a fast buck. Besides, half of the profits would be used to build the clinic.

The rationalization left a bad taste in her mouth.

The next item told her why. On the bill of sale, a small, cramped handwriting listed the lance's cost as five hundred dollars. Someone had added a zero to the purchase price. At the bottom of the document, Cheek had signed his name in the same cramped style. Beneath it the seller, Tillie Carwile, had shakily scrawled her name. By the sound of the woman's voice, Shea imagined her to be a gray-haired old lady with squinting, milky eyes. Either she hadn't seen the extra zero, or Cheek added it after she signed.

Shaking her head at the unfairness, Shea turned to the next document, the provenance verifying the history and authenticity of the lance. At the bottom of the paper were the signatures of Cheek, Cullen, and Tom Bennett.

She reached for Ann's Rolodex, thumbing through it until the card for the Santa Fe Museum popped up. A chirpy female voice answered the phone.

"Can I speak to Tom Bennett, please?"

"I'm sorry," Chirpy said, "he's not here."

"When will he be back?"

"Not until tomorrow. He flew to St. Louis. Can I take a message?"

"That won't be necessary. Thank you."

So, Bennett was on his way here, probably at the request of Lieutenant Jansen. Blade said last night the lance would be verified today. Who better to re-examine it than the man who joined in authenticating the relic the first time around. If Bennett declared it a fake, no other authority need be called in. If he claimed the relic was real, then Jansen could enlist another historian to confirm the claim. Bennett would have to give an authentic declaration or be caught.

The last piece of paper in the folder was the bill of sale between Cheek and the museum. Three thousand dollars! Quite a profit for Cheek. That and the money from the other relics would keep him in buckskin jackets and Bowie knives for quite a while. Ann signed as buyer.

Shea's spirits sank. If the lance was a fake, it now lay at Ann's doorstep, or it had been switched at the workshop. Things looked bad for Ann or Blade. Or both. Could they be partners? Was the affair between Ann and Cullen something Ann devised to distract him?

Footsteps echoed down the corridor. Shea stuffed the folder back in the drawer and closed it seconds before Cullen Gerard appeared at the door, his arm still in the satin sling.

"Well, well, well. What have we here?" he said.

She rose from the desk chair. "I dropped by to take Ann to lunch."

He eyed her dubiously. "As have I."

"She wasn't here."

"I see that."

He scanned the papers on the desk but seemed to relax at what he saw. Or didn't see. Was he looking for the folder she'd tucked into the bottom drawer?

"How's your arm?"

"I'll survive."

This cat and mouse game could go on all day. She decided to assume the part of the cat. "Is there something you need?" she asked, sorting through the papers. She watched his face for a sign of involvement.

"No, no." He tried to sound nonchalant, but tension edged his words.

She reached for the desk drawer. "I'm sure Ann wouldn't mind you looking for whatever you need."

Cullen darted behind the desk and caught her wrist. "That won't be necessary. Besides, I don't think Ann would want us mucking around in her desk."

Shea smiled and peered coyly into his eyes. "There are no secrets between Ann and me."

"What does that mean?"

"Ann told me all about the two of you." It was all she could think of to pierce his cool exterior. To rattle him enough to make a mistake.

His hold on her tightened. "Ann told you about us?"

"Of course. She tells me everything."

He stiffened, then let go of her. "Did she tell you about the powwow tonight?"

"I know about it."

"Good." He guided her to the hallway. "Ann and I will see you there."

He shut the door behind her and locked it.

Nineteen

Deep in thought, Shea descended the museum staircase. If Ann told the truth, Cullen hadn't been in Santa Fe with Cheek when someone murdered Ethan. However, he did have an alibi. He and Ann were in bed together. Either way, that took them both out of the running. So why did Cullen act so guilty?

Before she reached the bottom of the stairs, she ran into Blade. They stared at each other for a moment, then both spoke at once.

"Blade, I—"

"I was looking for—"

They laughed nervously.

"Ladies first," he said.

"No, you first."

"I'm looking for Ann Scott."

Shea's enthusiasm faded. She'd hoped he was looking for her, that he was ready to tell her the truth. The sight of him dressed in tux and war bonnet last night sent her blood rushing even now.

"Ann's not in her office."

"Then I guess you'll have to do," he said, grinning.

"Gee, thanks. Do for what?"

He laughed. "For lunch. I just had business to discuss with Ann."

He grasped her hand and pulled her behind him down the stairs. She had no time to protest. Caught up in his eagerness, she soon forgot about the disturbing note on which they'd parted the night before.

"Where're we going?" she asked as they walked across the museum grounds toward the parking lot.

He stopped next to a black Jeep Cherokee. "We got off to a bad start. I'm declaring a peace treaty. A halting of time. Nothing else exists—no suspicions, no half-truths, no mistrust—just you and me." He opened the Jeep door. "Will you come with me?"

Stay away from the Indians.

Lieutenant Jansen's admonition nagged at her, but if she hoped to find Ethan's killer, she needed more information. She hesitated only a moment, then slipped into the Jeep.

As soon as they settled in, Blade said, "Close your eyes."

"Now wait—"

"Trust me. Remember, we have a peace treaty."

Feeling guilty for possibly mistrusting an innocent man and for all the peace treaties broken by the white man, she took a deep breath and squeezed her eyes shut. "If I end up lost on a Dakota reservation somewhere..."

"Would that be so terrible? Lost with me?"

"I'll set aside my opinion until I see what I'm getting for lunch."

"On the reservation, we eat buffalo steaks fried in bear grease."

"Oh, please."

They traveled a short distance before the Jeep ground to a halt.

"Keep your eyes closed."

"Okay, okay."

He helped her out of the vehicle and along a paved path. Sunshine warmed her face. Children laughed nearby. A gate squeaked. Where was he taking her?

He halted and turned her away from him, his hands resting on her shoulders. "Okay, open your eyes."

Staring at her across a dry moat was the hugest grizzly bear she'd ever seen. "I'm not eating that."

"More likely he'd eat you." He spun her toward him. "It *is* feeding time at the zoo. Come on."

Blade bought hot dogs, fries, and soft drinks at the concession stand next to the seal pool and found a vacant bench. A zookeeper brought out a bucket of raw fish and tossed them one at a time over the water. Seals exploded upward in graceful, wet arcs, caught the fish, and splashed back into the pool. A crowd of school children dressed in plaid uniforms cheered.

As Shea bit into her hot dog, she decided she'd never eaten lunch in a more charming place or with a more charming, unpretentious man. A peacock strutted by, pausing to beg for something to eat. The bird bobbed its brightly colored head of blue and green feathers as it pecked at Shea's basket of fries sitting on the bench.

"I guess I'm done with those." She pushed the fries closer to the hungry bird. If someone told her a few days ago she'd be lunching at the zoo with seals, a peacock, and an Indian chief, she'd have called them crazy. When the bird lunged for her hot dog, Blade shooed it aside. Indignant, it strutted away, voicing its plaintive call that sounded like, "Help, help."

She grinned at Blade. "My hero."

He laughed. "Come on. I'll show you the animals and birds sacred to my people."

They strolled through the zoo hand in hand as he pointed out wolf and bison, eagle and hawk, elk and deer, and beaver, which the Indians once believed could think like men.

"The grizzly we saw earlier is the largest and fiercest of bears," he said. "A useful animal, it supplied the Indian with flesh, fat, and grease. We made moccasins from the skin and heavy fur robes to fight off the winter cold."

She was touched by the way he included himself when referring to his people, even those who lived long ago. They were a tribe neither time nor death could separate.

"We rubbed our bows with bear oil and strung them with bear gut," he continued. "The grizzly is Four Bears' totem. He wears a single bear claw around his neck."

She knew something about the grizzly. "I suppose you're aware that grizzlies are the only bears that can't climb trees."

"Fortunately, Indians can."

She laughed and laced her arm through his, gazing up into his face. How handsome he was. The sounds of the city, of people talking, and of animals keening faded away. They stood a moment in silence. He touched her cheek with the back of his hand, then leaned down and kissed her lightly on the lips.

You're a two-faced rat, McKenna. She'd forever remember their first real kiss was under false pretenses.

"Tell me more about your people," she said, brushing away the indignant voice hounding her. She should just ask her questions straight out, but that hadn't worked last night.

"The Sioux once lived in Minnesota." He pulled her down to sit with him in the shade of a large oak tree. "They eventually moved to the Great Plains. Seven Council Fires, as they called themselves, composed the Sioux Nation. Each had their own leader and language. The Teton Sioux speaks Lakota. The Yankton speaks Nakota. The Santee Sioux, my tribe, speaks Dakota. We have five principal religious rites. Sun Dance, Vision Cry, Ghost Keeper, Buffalo Chant, and Foster-parent Chant. All are intoned by a designated mythical person, *Pte-sa-vi ya.*"

"Te-sa what?" She stammered the difficult words.

"White Buffalo Woman."

"There's so much I don't know—that most of us don't know—about your people. About the entire Indian nation."

Self-reproach at why she'd agreed to come with him ate at her conscience. Even though she wanted to know him better, she also was trying to find a chink in his armor, a clue to his role in Ethan's death.

"All the tribes meet at least once a year in the summer, like the powwow tonight." He kissed her again. "You're coming, aren't you?"

"I wouldn't miss it." After a moment of silence—and some serious kissing—she said, "Then you'll be returning to the reservation to live." It wasn't a question. It was a statement of finality.

"For a while. At least until the clinic is finished."

And she would be on the other side of the world photographing the sacred white tigers of India or traveling in a gypsy wagon across the frozen tundra. She had her career. He had his responsibilities. Whatever this was between them, sadly she realized it could never last.

"Where have you two been?" Ann demanded as Shea and Blade strolled into the museum's foyer. "We've been looking everywhere for you." Worry lines creased her brow.

"What's going on?" Shea asked.

"Tom Bennett's here to verify the lance."

Blade tensed beside her and dropped her hand. The sense of loss stunned her.

"Then let's join them," he said.

The fatalistic tone of Blade's words sank Shea's heart. He looked as if he were walking his last mile as a free man.

She glanced at Ann who stared back with veiled emotions. Had Cullen told her he found Shea in her office—behind her desk? Seeing Shea and Blade hand-in-hand, did Ann doubt Shea's allegiance? Two days ago they were best friends, and she'd never heard of Blade Santee. Now, Shea had a terrible feeling she was about to lose both of them.

Upon entering the gallery, they found Cullen, Cheek, and Jansen huddled around a bespectacled man in khaki pants and an olive-drab shirt. No one spoke as he gently turned the lance over and over again in hands sheathed in white gloves.

Must be Tom Bennett.

"It's a fake." Bennett sniffed the lance. "Smells like it's been aged in tea."

Ann let out a strangled gasp.

Bennett returned the lance to the clear plastic evidence bag.

Cullen paled. "This is reprehensible." He grabbed for it. "Are you sure?"

"Of course, I'm sure," Bennett said in a peevish manner.

Cheek shouldered his way in. "How can you tell?"

"Remember, I've seen the original. Handled it. This is excellent work, but—it's fake."

"Where *is* the original?" Cullen snapped at no one in particular. He turned to Ann. "I want to see the paperwork."

Ann faltered and stepped back. "Of course."

"I could do carbon dating. It'll take time," Bennett offered. "There's something about it—it's a gut feeling, but it looks too—too fresh." He shook his head. "Tell you one thing, whoever did the work, he's good. Real good."

"This just can't be," Cullen said. "After the three of us verified the lance, it went straight to the Indians' workshop."

They all stared at Blade.

Shea held her breath, waiting for him to deny everything, but he remained mute, his eyes ablaze with resentment.

Bennett scanned the gallery. "Where are the other restored items? Let me check them."

Cullen strode to where the buffalo shield hung and slapped the wall next to it, anxiety etched on his face. Shea remembered how he'd fawned over the relic in the storeroom.

Bennett took a magnifying glass from his pocket and meticulously scrutinized the artifact. After a few minutes, he said, "The shield is authentic."

Cullen let out a sigh that Shea interpreted as relief.

Ann joined them and examined the shield.

"Well, that's good. That's good," Jansen said. "Maybe we've only got one forgery."

Cheek's eyes narrowed. He marched to a glass case where the Cheyenne necklace lay and brought it to Bennett. Shea recognized it as the one she'd tried on in the storeroom.

Everyone except Jansen flinched at Cheek's callous treatment of the relic.

"Careful. Careful," Bennett said and set to examining the bone pipes and beads. This, too, he declared authentic.

Cheek spun around and snatched an Arikara bone knife from the wall leading out of the gallery and shoved it at Bennett, who verified it as real, too.

"Cheek, I must protest," Cullen warned. "Be careful."

Cheek glared at Blade, his face a mask of restrained rage.

What was this between Blade and Cheek? The dealer should be happy the relics were real.

Shea glanced at Blade, his jaw set in a defiant line. All her doubts and fears about the Dakota chieftain came rushing back. She felt like a ping-pong ball, slammed back and forth between trusting and not trusting him.

Jansen removed a folded piece of paper from his jacket pocket. "I think we'll leave verifying the rest of the restored relics until we take a look at Santee's workshop. This is a warrant." He handed the document to Ann.

"I think that's an excellent idea," Cullen said with a tone of reproach aimed at Blade. He slowly twirled the fake lance in his hands.

Jansen stepped between the two men. "I'll take the lance, sir. It's still evidence in a murder investigation. And you, Mister Santee," Jansen turned to Blade. "You ride with me."

Cullen relinquished the lance but kept his eyes on Blade. "On Cheek's recommendation, I trusted you, Santee. I hope my faith wasn't misplaced. Someone has the real lance. Whoever's at fault, I plan to see he receives full punishment."

Cullen failed to mention something far more important: the murder of Ethan Brumley.

Twenty

At the workshop, the Indians were packing their artist's tools and supplies.

"Going someplace, boys?" Jansen asked as he ushered Blade into the room.

Shea and the rest followed. Officers Wolkalski, O'Reilly, and two uniforms took their post just inside the workshop door. The Dakotas stood back, staring first at Jansen, then at their chief.

"Our work here is done, Lieutenant," Blade said, defiance in his tone. "Only a few finished pieces remain to be taken to the museum and cataloged. We're returning to the reservation after the powwow tonight."

"Not quite," Jansen said. "No one's leaving town until I find Brumley's killer."

Shea flinched. That meant she'd have to delay leaving for Mexico. She'd never defaulted on an assignment before. As a freelancer, snapping great pictures and hitting the magazine's deadline determined whether or not she'd stay in business for long. Gram and Kathryn depended on her financial contribution.

Jansen pointed a stubby finger at Blade. "And you, sir, are now my prime suspect. If the real lance is on these premises—if we find anything suspicious, I'll be taking you downtown." He turned to his men. "Search the place."

The police proved thorough. No arrowhead or scrap of rawhide remained unturned. Cringing at their recklessness, Ann cautioned them to be careful even with the bits and pieces of artifacts.

With Bennett in tow, Jansen examined anything that remotely resembled an historical object or the remnant of one. Cullen stood aside, cold and aloof, anger roiling in his gray eyes. Stone-faced, Blade joined his men apart from the rest. Cheek continued to glare at him.

Disturbing thoughts raced through Shea's mind. All the evidence so far pointed to Blade's involvement in the forgery, if not Ethan's murder. Obviously, Cheek felt the same. Earlier today, as she and Blade talked and laughed and shared some drop-dead, earth-shaking kisses at the zoo, he gave no hint of his innocence or involvement. In fact, she had expected that to be the reason for their private little side trip and the main reason she'd agreed to go. Wrong again.

She avoided looking at him now, fearing he'd see mistrust in her eyes. Or worse, guilt.

"Lieutenant," one of the officers called. He was twisting the doorknob to the sleeping room. "This door's locked."

Apprehension swept over Shea. Blade had stopped Ann and her from entering that room the day they'd visited the workshop.

Jansen turned to Blade. "Open the door."

"There's nothing in there except Billy's personal things," Blade said. "It was his turn to stand guard this week." He nodded at his men. "We've all taken a turn."

Only Four Bears nodded back.

"You'll find all sorts of unimportant things in there," Blade added.

Had a signal passed between Blade and Four Bears? Had the real relics been hidden in the sleeping room, and Four Bears signaled he'd moved them? Her suspicious mind was working overtime.

Jansen showed no sign of backing down. "Then you won't object to my seeing."

Blade hesitated, then motioned to Billy. The young man unlocked the door. Everyone surged forward. Jansen stopped them at the doorway and stepped inside.

A neatly-made rollaway sat along the far wall. A suitcase partially filled with clothes lay atop the bed. The closet door stood ajar. Empty chest drawers hung open.

One of the officers searched under the bed. "Nothing here."

Shea heaved a sigh of relief. With all her heart, she wanted Blade to be innocent. But despite their failure to find hard evidence against him, things didn't look good. Even Cullen suspected him.

Disappointment clear, Jansen marched back into the workshop, pulling his characteristic baseball cap firmly on his head.

"Okay. So who delivered the lance to the museum?"

He seemed eager to wrap up the case and get back to homicides whose methods of murder were weapons of the twenty-first century.

Blade looked to Four Bears for the answer. The big Indian turned to Cheek. Cheek shook his head. A nervous voice answered from the doorway of the sleeping room.

"I did."

It was Billy, fear etched on his young face. Today he wore a T-shirt emblazoned with a Spanish galleon that resembled Columbus' Santa Maria. The caption beneath read "Go Home." Did his protesting of the white man's invasion go beyond T-shirts?

"Everyone went to lunch." He stared at Blade and Four Bears. "It was my turn to guard the relics. Remember, I asked you to bring me back a pizza?"

"Go on," Jansen said, fists balled on his hips.

"The old man—Mister Brumley—he called and said he needed more relics. He was done cataloging what he had."

Billy glanced at Blade again. "I know I wasn't supposed to leave the workshop, but he kept insisting I bring more relics. The lance was lying on your worktable," he said in a whisper. "Nothing else was finished, so I took it to him."

Shea didn't remember Billy delivering the lance, but she could've been in the restroom or at the soda machine.

"Then your fingerprints will be on the lance," Jansen said to Billy.

"I-I guess so," the young Indian stuttered, his head down. Shea could almost smell his panic.

"But when we dusted for prints, there were none." Jansen threw his hands into the air with exaggerated alarm. "Big surprise."

He glared at the group, turned, and walked to the workshop door. "Someone here knows more than they're telling," he called over his shoulder. "I'll be at the powwow tonight in case anyone wants to clear his conscience."

Shea surveyed the troubled faces of the others as they stared warily at one another.

For those who *have* a conscience, she thought.

Twenty-One

After the police left, Shea approached Blade. A shake of his head warned her away.

What was this? *Now* he wouldn't talk to her again?

He busied himself helping pack tools.

Her confusion turned to anger. Native American royalty aside, Blade's mercurial mood swings were too volatile for her, thank you very much. She'd finish her work, pack up her gear, and put the museum and Blade Santee far behind. She wondered how the weather was in Mexico this time of year.

On his way out the door, Cullen announced, "Cheek and I will drive Tom back to the museum to examine the remaining artifacts. Let's hope we find no more fakes."

Outside, Ann tugged at Shea's arm. "I need a drink."

"Let's go to my place," Shea offered, deciding it might be a good idea to discuss Blade's strange behavior with her friend—to set Ann's mind—and her own—at ease.

Imbibing in only an occasional glass of wine, Shea hadn't stocked her apartment with alcohol. In her estimate, a hot cup of chamomile tea—rather than Ann's scotch—would better soothe her friend's frazzled nerves. After the ordeal Jansen put them through and Blade's latest, unwarranted rejection, Shea could use a shot of chamomile herself. They were sitting at her kitchen table over steaming cups before either of them spoke again.

"I don't understand why Cheek acted so upset over a single forged relic," Shea said. "You'd think he'd be happy there weren't more."

Ann shook her head. "I think he's angry because he recommended Blade to Cullen. Blade forging the lance makes Cheek look bad."

"You seem to have Blade tried and convicted."

She'd hoped Ann would provide new information to clear Blade, not condemn him. As annoyed as she was, she couldn't bear the thought of him locked away in a prison cell the rest of his life.

Ann shrugged. "Either Blade or one of his tribesmen has to be guilty. You heard Billy. They had the lance last before it went to Ethan. What *can* I think?" She sipped her tea. "This is good."

Things looked bad for Blade and the Dakotas. As loyal as his men appeared, would they confess their guilt to him? Were they protecting him, or was he protecting one of them?

Shea stirred a teaspoonful of sugar into her tea. "Let's follow the lance through its restoration. How did the museum acquire it?"

She already knew, but the information needed to be on the table for scrutiny. If Cullen hadn't already snitched on her, she didn't want Ann to know she'd been searching through her desk for evidence of malfeasance. Another guilt trip for suspecting her friend galloped over Shea's horizon.

Ann related the lance's provenance and journey to the museum, confirming what Shea had learned. "I was shocked to see how little Cheek paid the woman," Ann finished.

Shea was glad to hear that.

"Five hundred dollars."

She wasn't glad to hear that. Tillie Carwile received a measly fifty.

"Of course, the museum has no control over Cheek," Ann said, "or how he conducts his business."

Shea waited for an explanation of Ann's cavalier attitude. Cheek had lied about the price of the lance. He'd cheated an old woman out of her fair share. A man was dead. According to Lieutenant Jansen, prison loomed on the horizon for Blade and his accomplice. Her career and Ann's were on the line. And Shea's feelings for a suspected murderer were twisting her into a confused pretzel. But Ann offered no explanation for her laissez-faire position.

"How'd you meet Cheek?" Shea asked.

"Through Cullen. He made purchases from the dealer when he'd worked for other museums. They have a long-standing relationship. That's why Cullen can't believe Cheek's involved." She paused. "Cheek gives me the creeps, but Cullen says he's never had a problem with him. On the other hand, we know little about Blade."

Ann peeked at Shea over the rim of her teacup. "You seem to be progressing in that area. First, I catch you necking in the diorama's tepee. Then waltzing on the terrace at the Patrons Ball."

Shea hadn't been aware anyone saw them dancing.

Ann answered her quizzical look. "Through the gallery windows. And holding hands today in the museum foyer."

No wonder she'd cast a suspicious glance in Shea's direction earlier. Her friend probably questioned Shea's loyalty. Shea wasn't too sure herself. She sipped her tea again, the calming liquid working its magic. Ann seemed more relaxed, too.

"Okay, so now the lance is back at the museum," Shea continued, leaning back in the kitchen chair. "Whose idea was it to call in Bennett for a third verification?"

"Cullen's."

"Had he worked with the man before?"

"No, but everyone on the museum circuit knows of Tom Bennett. He's the best at verifying Indian relics."

Shea never heard of him before Ethan informed her, proof she spent too much time out of the country. Maybe she should concentrate more on American vistas. Like a Dakota reservation.

"Then Bennett wasn't selected because he's a close friend of Cullen's or Cheek's?" she asked.

"No, but Cullen insisted on using him."

"Insisted?"

"Well, yes. He said he'd only work with those best in their field of expertise. Like Cheek. He's unbelievably good at finding relics. And Blade's the most prominent artisan to restore them. Cullen's reputation is at stake if anyone on his team fails to perform in a top-notch manner."

"So we have to concede that at the point of verification here in St. Louis the lance was authentic."

"Yes," Ann agreed. "Unless Bennett's involved with Blade."

Shea nearly choked on a mouthful of tea. "Blade?"

"Sure. Bennett's from the Santa Fe Museum of Antiquities. Blade has a studio in Santa Fe. It stands to reason the top authenticator of Native American artifacts would cross paths with the number one restorer."

Rats! There's that practicality she admired in Ann.

"You're saying Blade and Bennett could have perpetrated the scam?"

"When Bennett, Cullen, and Cheek authenticated the relics," Ann said, obviously warming to the idea of Blade and Bennett in alliance, "Cullen allowed Bennett to make his determination first. He was the visiting authority. It's protocol."

"And even if Cullen or Cheek thought they detected something amiss," Shea finished for Ann, "they might not admit it in the face of a world expert on the subject."

Ann nodded. "That's altogether possible."

"But why have three people verify the relics if they're not going to be truthful?"

"Cullen and Cheek were being truthful as far as they knew. They could've been intimidated by Bennett's expertise and didn't want to look ridiculous contradicting him. Who would arbitrate the matter? Bennett's decisions are respected as the final word."

"I see what you mean." Even in the area of relics, however, Shea couldn't fathom anyone intimidating Cullen or Cheek. "So what happened next?"

"Cheek, Blade, or one of the other Indians then took the artifacts to Blade's workshop. Once there, they were under the craftsmen's care."

"And Billy delivered the lance to Ethan."

"Barbara was to register the artifacts after they came back from Blade. But she took ill before she even started. I called in Ethan. Then I hired you, and you know the rest."

Shea still didn't want to accept Blade as a murderer. "Who worked on the lance?"

Ann arched a brow. "I never thought to ask. Blade's in charge of the workshop. I can't imagine his men forging an artifact without his authorization or knowledge. Besides, Billy said the lance had been lying on Blade's workbench."

Shea swallowed another gulp of tea, hoping it would make this scenario go down easier. Blade could've known about the forgery but kept his mouth shut. That didn't mean he knew anything about Ethan's murder. She took a deep breath before she asked her next question.

"What time did Cullen come to the museum to take you to dinner?"

Ann thought for a moment. "I'd just returned from the ladies room and locked my office to leave."

Ethan had asked Shea the time—midnight—before he went to Ann's office. "So Cullen met you in your office around midnight?"

"No. I ran into Cullen at the back door. I guess the guard let him in."

"He was alone?"

"Yes. He said he was coming up to see if I'd had dinner. I said I was famished, but I needed to go to the storeroom to tell you and Ethan to quit for the night. Cullen said that wouldn't be necessary, because you'd leave when you tired or were finished working."

How thoughtful of Cullen. After he'd told everyone to work day and night on the tight deadline, he was planning a late night dinner and a romp between the sheets with Ann.

"How long have you known Cullen?"

"Only since he went to work for the Gateway Historical Society a few months ago. Why?" Ann's words turned huffy.

"Nothing. Just wondered how well you knew him beyond his professional accolades."

"Better than you know Blade."
Touché.
"And Cullen was with you for the rest of the night?"
"Till seven Friday morning." Ann's words remained guarded. "I showered and dressed. We parted. I came to the museum, only to be greeted by the sight of Ethan's body lying on the lawn." Her voice softened. "It was horrible."

"And Cullen?"

"He left my apartment when I did. Said he was going home to shower and change clothes. Like he told Lieutenant Jansen, he saw the commotion as he drove by the museum and came in to see what was wrong." Ann pinned Shea with a probing glare. "Where were you and Blade this morning?"

"Uh, we went to the zoo."

"To the zoo? Why?"

"For lunch. To get to know each other better."

"Did you? Get to know him better?"

There was insinuation in Ann's question. Shea deserved that. Turnabout is fair play, but it can be the pits.

"I went to the Ball alone last night," she answered, "and I came home alone. Today, I met Blade climbing the stairs to the museum's second floor around noon. He said he was looking for you. I informed him you weren't in your office. He asked me to go with him. I thought he might want to tell me—"

She wrestled with the best way to word what she said next. "To tell me something of value concerning all that's been going on. We had lunch at the zoo. We then returned to the museum where we ran into you in the foyer. I learned nothing about Ethan's death or Blade's involvement. I do know that in my gut, I don't believe he's a murderer."

"Nor I, Cullen," Ann said.

Shea smiled to appease her friend. "Then let's move on. Where did Cheek go that night after he and Cullen returned from Santa Fe?"

A puzzled frown crossed Ann's face. "I don't know."

Something flashed in her eyes. A revelation?

"What?" Shea asked, her interest mounting.

"It's nothing I suppose, but I don't remember seeing Cullen's car in the parking lot. He walked me straight to my car. We were talking about the Anasazi pottery, got in, and left."

Shea wondered if Cullen or Cheek saw Bennett while they were in Santa Fe. Maybe there'd never been any pottery. The trip was a ruse to get to Bennett and plan strategy to cover their tracks. *If* they were in cahoots. Or threaten him if they weren't. Ann seemed to think Cullen knew Bennett only by reputation.

"What kind of car does Cullen drive?"

"A silver Bentley."

Shea didn't recall seeing a silver car in the museum parking lot the night she sprinted to her Blazer. Ann's red MG wasn't there either.

"What kind of car did Ethan have?"

"Oh, Ethan doesn't—didn't have a car. He relied on the kindness of friends or public transportation. He often rode the MetroLink. There's a station across from the museum at DeBaliviere Boulevard and Forest Park Expressway."

Shea guessed the remaining four cars in the museum parking lot belonged to the guard and cleaning crew. Had one belonged to the murderer?

"What does Cheek drive?" she asked.

"I don't know. I know very little about him. I'd rather keep it that way."

Shea hadn't realized remembering the cars would be important. But one car now stood out in her mind, because she saw it recently. A black Jeep Cherokee. Blade had been on the museum grounds the night Ethan died. And Cheek had not been in Santa Fe.

"I better get back," Ann said. "God forbid, but Bennett might have found more forged artifacts."

"I have a few items to photograph for the catalogs."

Ann paused. "Maybe you shouldn't see Blade—socially—until this whole thing blows over. If he's a murderer, it could be dangerous. And if he's only guilty of fraud, it doesn't look good for the museum or you to be seen together."

It was Shea's turn to bristle. "I could say the same for you and Cullen."

Ann stuck her hand out. "Then it's a pact. We avoid being alone with the guys until this is cleared up."

Shea reached across the table and shook Ann's hand. "Deal."

When they stood, Ann pointed to the jacket with leather elbow patches hanging on one of the kitchen chairs. "Is that Ethan's?"

Shea picked up the tweed coat. "The night he died, I brought it to your office to save him a trip back to the storeroom. When I couldn't find either of you, I accidentally brought it home with me. I guess we should give it to Lieutenant Jansen."

"I'll do it." Ann picked up their teacups and saucers and carried them to the kitchen sink.

"Thanks." Shea wanted to avoid the lieutenant, but she couldn't help wondering why Ann was so eager to take Ethan's coat.

Good heavens, McKenna, you're becoming paranoid.

When she laid the jacket next to Ann's purse, she heard a crinkling sound.

Ann still stood at the sink, her back turned, rinsing teacups.

Shea eased a scrap of paper from the pocket. She recognized Ethan's familiar scrawl from the catalog sheets.

Blade Santee is involved.
Must talk to him.

Before Ann turned around, Shea slipped the note into her jean pocket.

Twenty-Two

Unanswered questions troubled Shea as she returned to the storeroom. Although Blade and his men alibied each other, his actions were erratic. She still didn't know who was lying about Cullen's whereabouts that night. She wanted to believe Ann, but she needed to be objective. In love with Cullen, her friend had become so concerned about his safety she was packing a gun. Who knew what the besotted curator might do to protect him.

On the other hand, Shea doubted anything Cheek said. Quoting Ann's sentiments, the man gave her the creeps. She shouldn't judge people without getting to know them, but something about him rang false. He certainly didn't seem like anyone the aristocratic Cullen Gerard would associate with, even for business reasons. Ethan and Blade's obvious dislike for the dealer only reinforced her mistrust. How would she ever be able to question him about Ethan's death?

She didn't have long to wonder. Upon entering the museum storeroom, she found Cheek groping through the relics.

"Hello," she said, steeling herself as she walked to the opposite side of the workbench.

Cheek wore his trademark buckskin jacket, unsuitably hot for this time of year, but useful for hiding weapons beneath. He smelled of soured sweat. Grunting a hello, he fingered a medicine pipe and a ceremonial mask representing a Manitou lying on the table. She didn't know whether the fabled Manitou was a good spirit or bad, but the mask's black scraggly hair, bared teeth, and wild eyes suggested the latter. She found it disconcerting how much it resembled Cheek.

His ham hock of a hand came to rest on the hilt of his Bowie knife. With the other hand, he made a sweeping motion over the relics. "Mr. Gerard says to photograph all these. Someone will catalog them later for inventory."

She waved her fingers over the mask. "This is excellent work. So intricate and detailed. Did you do this?"

"No."

"Anyone other than an expert would have difficulty telling where the original work ceased and the repairs began." Was she being too obvious?

"Santee and his men know their business."

To what business was he referring? Relic restoration or forgery? Or murder?

"You've known Blade for a while?" She tried to make her questions conversational. He wouldn't hold still for an out and out interrogation.

"Been in his Santa Fe studio a few times," he mumbled and headed toward the door. "I've got work to do."

She wasn't finished questioning him yet. Propelling herself around the workbench, she cut him off. So much for subtlety.

Her heart pounded in her throat as she held her ground between the big Indian—half Indian—and freedom. "So you and Blade are only working acquaintances?"

He didn't answer.

She pressed on. "And Cullen? Have you worked with him very long?"

With each word, Cheek's hold on the knife tightened.

She swallowed hard and repeated to herself that they were in a public place. Surely, he wasn't stupid enough to hurt her here. The knowledge that Ethan died just outside these walls didn't help. She glanced around at the packing crates that surrounded them. If Cheek chose to kill her, it'd be a while before anyone would find her knife-mutilated body.

She pushed the unsettling thought from her mind. "Cullen vouched for you," she continued. "You and he have worked together for some time."

"That's right," Cheek answered in a cautious tone.

She'd have to dig out every piece of information with the stubbornness of a dog gnawing marrow from a bone.

"Does that mean you found relics for him at other institutions where he worked?"

He drew himself up to his full height and towered menacingly over her five feet six inches. If he was trying to intimidate her, he was doing an excellent job.

Smirking, he said, "I don't have to answer your questions. You're not the law."

"If you've nothing to hide, why would you mind?"

He wagged his broad head like an enraged bull. His knife hand shifted back and forth on the hilt as if he were cutting out someone's heart. Probably hers.

Despite the cold knot forming in her stomach, Shea stood her ground. It was the only way to find out what Cheek knew.

"You better go play with your camera." His words held an unspoken threat.

Or what? You'll do to me what you did to Ethan?

The image of Ethan's poor twisted body pinned to the ground with the lance caused her to falter. She breathed deeply, steadying her nerve, and asked the next question. If he chose not to answer, then that was that. She'd done the best she could.

"Were you at the museum the night Ethan was murdered?"

"I was in Santa Fe with Cullen." Cheek growled his response, despite his vow not to answer. "You heard us tell Jansen that in the conference room."

"But Ann says Cullen was with her from midnight on. What kind of car do you drive?" She fired the questions and rebuttals at him as fast as she could to keep him off balance.

He seemed puzzled by the question. "A pickup. What has that got to do with anything?"

"A tan pickup?"

She couldn't suppress her excitement. The memory of the four vehicles parked outside the museum that night came flooding back: a dark-colored sedan, a white van with lettering, Blade's black Jeep, and a tan pickup.

"Yeah, a tan pickup."

"Did you drive Cullen to the museum?"

Realizing he'd placed himself at the murder scene, his sweaty face warped into a grotesque mask like that of the Manitou. He moved closer, dwarfing her. Again she recalled Jansen's warning to stay away from the Indians. Somehow, she'd never felt intimidated by the others. Even Four Bears' adamant stand concerning ownership of the relics hadn't frightened her.

On the other hand, Cheek had made her uneasy since the day they'd met. She must be crazy confronting him alone. Her concern for Ann and Blade had replaced her common sense.

Instinctively, she backed away.

He kept coming, a murderous intent imprinted on his face, until he backed her against the wall. His jowls quivered with rage. His thick lips worked as if he were saying terrible things to her, but no words came out. It was an irrational thought, but she hoped he'd kill her quickly without touching her. She couldn't stand the thought of his hands on her.

At that moment, Blade carried two restored artifacts into the room. A rawhide shield in one hand, a tomahawk in the other. Anger flashed like summer lightning in his eyes when he took in the scene. Quick as a puma, he stepped between them. "What's going on?"

All Shea saw from behind Blade were his broad shoulders and alert stance. His back muscles tensed. His left hand grasped the shield more firmly. In his right hand, the tomahawk raised ever so slightly at his side.

"I was looking at some relics," Cheek said. "Checking to see if they're fake or real."

She peeked around Blade. Cheek seemed to have shrunken a bit.

"Then your business here is finished." Blade's hold on the tomahawk visibly tightened.

Cheek's hand fell away from the Bowie knife. He glared at Shea. "I'm done—for now."

She didn't like the sound of that. Blade must not have either. As soon as Cheek left, the Dakota chieftain turned his anger on her. "Stay away from Cheek."

"I beg your pardon."

Was he giving her orders? Too much was at stake for her to leave one stone unturned, even if it was a mean, nasty, murderous boulder carrying a Bowie knife.

Blade shook his head. "I don't know what was going on here, but Cheek's no one to mess with."

She folded her arms across her chest. "I assure you I do not enjoy *messing* with Cheek. Ann and I—and you—are under suspicion for murder. I have a right to do some investigating on my own."

She wasn't about to tell him Jansen no longer considered her a suspect, and that her main concern was for Ann and him. If he didn't trust her enough to confess his role in all this, she'd find out for herself.

She also wasn't about to tell him the little display of male testosterone between him and Cheek had sent heat rippling through her.

"Do you trust me?" he asked, as if he'd read her mind.

"I don't know."

"You need to trust me."

She looked away. She wanted to trust him, but his refusal to confide in her kept getting in the way. If *he* didn't trust her, how could she trust *him*?

"Leave the investigating to the police," he said. "That's their job. Yours is photographing relics." He laid the shield and tomahawk on the workbench. "Stay away from Cheek."

She could suppress her frustration no longer. "What are you afraid of?"

He shook his head. "There are things you don't understand."

She leaned against the workbench. "You're absolutely right. So help me."

He glanced at the doorway. "It wouldn't be safe for you to know."

"Safe for whom? You asked me to trust you. You need to trust me. I'll try to help."

"You can't help. There's no help for me." The fatalistic tone of his voice tore at her heart.

"But—"

He grabbed hold of her, his strong fingers painfully digging into the soft flesh of her arms. He pressed his lips against her temple. "Just promise me you'll stay away from Cheek."

When she didn't answer, he released her and strode out the door.

She was left to contemplate a niggling question. Was Blade trying to protect her from Cheek, or was he afraid she might find out something to incriminate *him*?

Twenty-Three

Shaken from her run-in with Cheek, Shea ran to the ladies room and splashed cold water on her face. The distressing certainty that Blade might have more to do with Ethan's murder than she cared to think about didn't help. She'd hoped discovering additional information would clarify things.

Wrong.

After slipping a Pepsi from the soda machine in the hallway, she hurried back to the storeroom. It was getting late and she had a workbench full of relics to photograph.

Nearing the storeroom door, she heard activity in the supply room at the end of the hall. Maybe it was Joe, the janitor she'd met the night Ethan died. He might know something about the murder. She found him filling his utility cart with cleaning products.

"Joe, remember me?"

She rested a hand on the cart so he couldn't get away without dragging her along. So far, the people she'd questioned had been reluctant if not downright hostile when she approached them.

"Yeah, you're the girlie who was lookin' for Missus Scott the other night." He jammed a mop into the cart.

She frowned. Ann was "Missus Scott" and Shea was a "girlie" to this man. Just goes to show you how signing someone's paycheck instilled respect.

"That's right. You said you'd seen Ann Scott and an old man. Separately."

"Yeah, that's right."

She assumed the old man Joe referred to was Ethan, but she better make sure. "What'd the elderly gentleman look like?"

"A squirrelly little guy carrying a spear."

Ethan.

"Did you see anyone else that night?"

Joe scratched the back of his neck and grimaced, as if it hurt him to think. "Yeah. The guard at the door when me and my crew come in."

"Did you and your crew come to work in separate cars?"

"Nah. I've got a white company van that I haul all of us and our equipment in."

Good. Three vehicles accounted for and one to go. Of course, it was possible the killer didn't drive to the museum. Maybe he walked over from the workshop or from the encampment of RVs, tents, and tepees. Or, like Ethan, rode the MetroLink.

"Did you see anyone else?"

"Yeah, two of them Indians."

"Two?"

"Yeah, they was together. In the new gallery. I was in the hallway, dusting. They didn't notice me. Nobody notices the cleaning crew. It's like we're invisible. Like we're part of the fixtures." He sounded as if his feelings were hurt.

"Hey, Joe, I remembered you," she said.

He smiled a lopsided grin. "Yeah, you did. That's nice."

She also remembered she saw two shadowy figures by the gallery's entrance that night.

"What did these men look like?"

"The Indians? They was big and had long hair down their back."

That eliminated Billy Quintella, who was slight and had a standard men's cut. It also eliminated Cheek whose shaggy black hair skimmed his collar. At least he wasn't one of the two men Joe saw in the gallery, but Cheek had been there. She'd seen his tan pickup.

"I remember somethin' else," Joe added. "One of 'em wore a

red feather in his hair. I could barely see with just the light from the hallway—with no lights on in the gallery—but I got good eyesight. Better'n 20-20. I was a sniper in Iraq," he said with pride.

So Blade and another Indian had been in the museum the night Ethan died. Why in the dark? And no one saw Ethan after Joe saw him outside Ann's office. No one except the murderer.

"What were they doing, Joe? The Indians."

"They was doin' somethin' with the stuff on the walls. Puttin' somethin' up or takin' it down, I'm not sure which."

"When was this?"

"After midnight." He looked at her as if she'd jog his memory. "But before I saw you."

She recalled her encounter with the imaginary bogeyman in the basement hallway that turned out to be her own reflection. Now she wasn't so sure. Had there been someone else there? Maybe one of the Indians was keeping an eye on her while another was outside killing Ethan. Her heart ached to think such a thing.

Blade and one of his men were in the museum that night. Ann and Cullen had been there. Joe, his cleaning crew, and the guards were making their usual rounds. With all the work going on, the guards had probably been given a list of who was allowed in the museum while closed. If she could find someone else who'd seen Cheek or his pickup in the parking lot, then she'd have corroboration he had been there, too. No sense in asking Joe. Cheek and Cullen hadn't returned from Santa Fe yet when the cleaning crew arrived.

She asked anyway. "Think your crew might have seen or heard something?"

He shook his head. "My crew is me and three other guys. Cops questioned all of us. I was the only one working in this wing. And now you know everything I know about that night."

Shea turned loose of the utility cart. "You've been a big help, Joe."

A big help in putting a noose further around Blade's neck.

Twenty-Four

This whole affair was making Shea crazy. The more she tried to help Blade, the more evidence she generated against him. His attitude and failure to trust her didn't help. She found it difficult to concentrate on her work. Struggling with the last few photo shots, she finished in disgust. Luckily, as inventory records, they'd end up in the museum's vault, away from critical eyes.

Still, whatever job she did, she did it to the best of her ability. She allowed nothing, absolutely nothing, to compromise the integrity of her work. Not tight schedules. Not sickness. Not her fear of heights. Not an over-wrought squid backed into a watery corner or the monsoon season in Lumpur. She darn well wasn't about to start now.

Angry and frustrated, she packed up her equipment and carted it to the Blazer. The same museum guard held open the vestibule door. Maybe he knew something that would clear Blade. Failing miserably so far, she understood the despair she'd seen in the chieftain's eyes.

On the last trip to her car, she paused in the vestibule doorway. "Could you help me with something else?"

The guard gave her a courteous nod. "What would that be, ma'am?"

Well, at least now she was a "ma'am" and not a "girlie."

"The night Ethan Brumley died, I left late," she said to jog his memory. "About one-thirty in the morning."

"Yes, ma'am, I remember."

"Did anyone leave after me?"

"Just the cleaning crew. And the Indians."

"How many Indians?"

"Two. Blade Santee and one of his men. They brought restored relics."

"Did you see Cheek Larson?"

"No ma'am."

Why would Blade take the relics to the gallery? They were to come to the storeroom to be cataloged and photographed.

"Who left between midnight and the time I went home?"

"The office crew got off at five and the cleaning crew came in, then left after you. Right after the Indians. No one else came or went through the front door."

"You said that night Ann Scott left by the back door."

"Must have. She didn't leave through here. Someone punches in the alarm code, back door opens. Only a few minutes to walk through. Then it closes and re-locks before the alarm resets. Look."

He showed her the security panel with rows of numbers like a calculator by the front door.

"Who besides Ann knows the code?"

"The security team that opens up and closes. That's all."

It wasn't an elaborate system. The building had been erected by 1913 with money earned from the 1904 St. Louis World's Fair. The alarms were probably added much later.

"What kind of car do you drive?" she asked.

"A dark blue Chevy. Bill, the guard in the other wing, and I ride together. Sometimes we take my car, sometimes his. That night I drove."

That, more than likely, was the fourth vehicle she saw in the parking lot. She remembered it was a dark color, but she didn't know a Chevy from a Fig Newton. Most cars looked the same to her, except for little sports cars like Ann's red MG. She could, however, tell a dark blue car from a black Jeep from a tan pickup from a white van. That accounted for the four vehicles in the parking lot. Ann's red MG and Cullen's silver Bentley hadn't been there. Cullen could've ridden to the museum from the airport with Cheek, then departed with Ann.

So that left the cleaning crew, the guards, Cheek, Blade, and possibly one of the other Indians in the museum when Shea went home. And, of course, Ethan—alive or already dead.

Did Blade and one of his men overpower the old registrar? Did Cheek join them in snuffing out their "thorn in the flesh" or did he act alone? The dealer could have been lurking somewhere on the grounds when Shea walked to her car. Or, hidden by darkness, killing Ethan at that very moment. The thought sent a wave of nausea through her.

"Do you think the other guard saw anything?"

"Bill? No ma'am. Not from his side of the building. That's what he told the police."

Shea doubted Bill would tell her anything new. If she dug up something later disproving that, she'd retrace her steps.

Bidding goodnight to the guard, she trudged deep in thought to her car. Blade's erratic behavior and the hopelessness in his voice plagued her. It seemed the more she tried to help, the more she discovered damning evidence to convict him. She felt like she was sinking in quicksand. Every bit of information she uncovered drug her deeper into the pit, and she was dragging Blade down with her.

Maybe she'd find the answers she needed at the powwow.

Twenty-Five

Shea could hear the drums.

They'd been thrumming their hypnotic cadence for over an hour. Remembering her encounter with Cheek in the museum storeroom, she had second thoughts about going to the powwow. She took his last words as a threat. What if she ran into him again—alone?

She found it hard to resist the tom-tom's insistent summons.

At the Patrons Ball last night, Blade laughed and danced and flirted with her. He refused, however, to answer her questions about his role in forging the war lance as if he didn't care what she thought. Earlier today at the zoo, he was charming and affectionate, but stood apart from her during Tom Bennett's examination of the lance. Later, in the storeroom, Blade rescued her from an enraged Cheek, even though during the police's search of his workshop, he'd turned a cold shoulder.

No doubt about it. Blade confused and disappointed her. By the time she arrived back at her apartment tonight, she'd decided to avoid the Dakota chieftain until she learned who killed Ethan. Every time they met, their encounter turned disastrous.

And she'd made a pact with Ann to keep away from Blade.

Nope, she wasn't going to the powwow. She'd stay right here in the carriage house and fix herself a cup of tea. It worked earlier to calm Ann; it'd work for her now.

But the drums kept calling. She made every effort to ignore them, including lingering in the shower to drown out the compelling sound until she resembled a prune.

"You're a photographer, not a detective," she told her reflection in the bathroom mirror. "Mind your own business."

Problem was she'd have no business to mind if she couldn't concentrate on her work. She couldn't concentrate, however, if Ethan's death and Blade's touch haunted her every thought.

Peering into her closet, she wondered what one wore to a powwow. If she were going to a powwow. Which she wasn't.

"You're the Rock of Gibraltar," she murmured, deciding on stonewashed jeans, boots, and a blue western-yoked calico blouse. She blow-dried her hair and secured it with the blue and white headband Blade had given her.

After dabbing on mascara and a hint of mauve lipstick, she threw her keys, money, and five rolls of unexposed film into a fanny pack and strapped it around her hips. She'd planned to add her cell phone—in case she needed to call the cavalry for help—but it was out of juice.

Grabbing her camera, she headed for the door. She wouldn't look so suspicious asking questions about Blade and his men if she snapped pictures of the ceremony. She could always claim to be covering the powwow for *Anthropology Today*. If her efforts to find clues proved fruitless, she'd have photos to sell. Already her hands felt steadier.

The powwow's drums boomed loudly across the street on the other side of the forest. Cars, pickups, and SUVs were parked bumper to bumper down Skinker Boulevard. She couldn't have found a space any closer than her own alleyway, so she decided to walk.

A full moon shone overhead as she skirted the woods. Stars twinkled, vying for dominance with the city lights. She followed the sound of drums to the cluster of campers, tents, and tepees. Posted signs announced the St. Louis Indian Society sponsored the event and prohibited the use of drugs or alcohol in the area. As she dashed past a tepee, a man in full Indian regalia stepped out, nearly colliding with her.

"Oh, excuse me." She halted, taken aback by his strange markings.

Chalky white paint covered the lower half of his face. The

upper half was kohl black. A gray-brown coyote headdress with dead amber eyes hunkered low over his forehead. Tufts of black, white, and brown turkey feathers festooned the crown. Dressed in black, the Indian wore a feathered crow bustle fanned out behind him that rustled like dry leaves when he moved. She noticed a sheathed knife strapped to his hip and another tucked into his knee-high buckskin moccasins.

He stared back, not responding.

She started to apologize again, but the scowl on his vaguely familiar face stopped her. Unnerved, she hurried on.

Beyond the tepees, she came to the booths where Indians sold their handcrafted wares. People jostled to purchase reed baskets, clay pottery, and brightly-colored blankets. Women fingered beaded purses, headbands, and pouches, looking for something to match their outfits. Men bartered for hand-tooled leather belts, moccasins, and knife sheathes. Her mouth watered when she passed a booth selling sweet-smelling fry bread.

She came to a huge circle of serape-covered benches. Its opening pointed east. In the center, a bonfire blazed while several Indian men pummeled a large drum with feathered beaters. Men, women, and children wearing buckskins, satins, and furs danced around the drum, always keeping it to their right. They stepped down on their right toe first, then lowered their heel with a thump. Then the left toe and heel. Thump. Toe. Heel. Thump. Toe. Heel. Thump. Around they danced as one of the drummers chanted in his native tongue.

She didn't see Blade or any of his men among the dancers. Searching the throng of spectators, she recognized Billy Quintella outside the circle's entrance. The young Indian wore jeans, moccasins, a yellow calico shirt with gold ribbons sewn along the yoke line and cuffs, colorful glass beads around his neck, and no feathers. He bounced excitedly from foot to foot as if this was his first powwow, too.

Even with his back to her, there was no mistaking the gorgeous hunk of Indian standing next to Billy. Broad shoulders.

Tapered waist. Taut thighs. Yep, Blade Santee.

She was surprised to see him wearing the same clothes he'd worn earlier—black jeans and a shirt. She expected him to be decked out in magnificent regalia befitting a future chief. Even so, his presence had drawn the attention of every Indian maiden within a ten-mile radius. They hovered around him like humming birds seeking nectar.

A twinge of jealousy gathered momentum inside her.

Okay, can that.

Taking a deep breath, she sauntered up to the group with a casual air that denied her pounding pulse. No matter how many times she saw him, he left her breathless. Cooler heads would have to prevail if she were to gather clues.

"Hello, Billy," she said. "Blade."

Blade turned, and she caught a fleeting glimpse of excitement in his eyes. "I'm glad you came," he said.

The gaggle of giggling Indian girls insinuated themselves between her and Blade before she could respond. They bombarded him with questions. Was he married? Where was he from? What tribe did he belong to? How long was he staying in the area?

Blade held up his hands in surrender. "I have to go now. Prepare myself for my dance in the Sacred Circle."

The girls moaned their regrets.

He looked pointedly at Shea. "I want to talk to you, but not now. Billy will show you around."

Blade faded into the crowd.

Disappointment clouded Billy's face as the girls dispersed.

"Having a good time?" Shea asked, hoping he wasn't so crestfallen he'd refuse to answer her questions.

His frown spread into an infectious grin. "Oh, yeah." He eyed her camera. "Will you take a picture of me dancing in the circle?"

"I'd be glad to. Why don't we take some now?"

His demeanor turned serious as he struck a grandiose pose. She restrained a smile, snapping pictures while she asked questions.

"I've never been to a powwow. How does it work?"

Billy answered eagerly. "At the beginning, the ringmaster says a prayer, then the procession into the Sacred Circle begins. Here." He pointed to the opening in the arc of benches. "The Head Man Dancer carrying the Indian Society's Eagle Staff enters, then the Head Woman Dancer. Behind them come the men dancers, starting with the Fancy Dancers, the Straight Dancers—they wear no feathers—and the Buckskin Dancers. Next comes the women Fancy Dancers and Shawl Dancers. And then the children."

She got shots of the various groups he'd named.

"So there's a specific order?"

"Oh, yes. And no one can dance except an Indian who knows the ways of the Sacred Circle, or someone invited by an Indian who will watch over him."

"Or her."

"Yeah, or her," Billy agreed. He pointed at Shea's jeans. "You couldn't dance in the Circle in pants. You'd have to tie a shawl around your waist. Women wear skirted outfits and a shawl draped around their shoulders or over their arm."

"I see." She snapped a picture of two Indian women passing by.

Billy smoothed his hands over his clothes. "The feathers and material and colors have special meaning. Northern Indians like the Seneca or the Chippewa wear skins and fur. Southern Indians like the Seminole, Navajo, or Apache wear cloth, like satin or calico."

She saw the logic in that. Temperatures in different regions dictated the appropriate clothing.

"White in the dressing," he said, "can mean the direction north or thanksgiving or the White Buffalo Calf Woman who gave the Sioux our Sacred Pipe. Black means healing. Blue is the color of the eagle. Red, green, and yellow are directions on the compass. Yellow's also the color of the elk, love, virility, and courtship."

Captivated, she stopped taking pictures and looked closer at the Indians' outfits as they passed by.

"And the feathers?"

"The eagle feather signifies strength. The hawk, vision. The wearer of these feathers receives the bird's power. An Indian must earn feathers."

He nodded at the dancers. "And when he is fancy dancing, spinning and leaping, it's the women's responsibility to stay out of his way. So as not to touch his feathers.

"If a feather drops, everything stops. There must be a ceremony immediately restoring the feather and its power to the dancer. It's a religious thing."

"Fascinating."

"There are many types of dances, each with its own purpose," Billy continued. "The Buffalo Dance was once performed to ensure a good hunt and to honor the animal that was a totem as well as a clan symbol. He was believed to instruct the medicine man on where to find healing plants and herbs. There's the Medicine Dance, Rain Dance, Snake Dance, and Sun Dance, and more, all with a special goal."

The drumming stopped and the dancers left the Circle. An announcer called for a break so the drummers could eat dinner and refresh themselves.

"I gotta go, too," Billy said. "I promised some new friends I'd meet them for fry bread. Hope you enjoy the powwow."

"Thanks, Billy."

Alone once more, Shea consoled herself with the fact that Blade had asked to talk with her later. Knowing how she felt, his request could only mean one thing. He was ready to tell her the truth.

Twenty-Six

Shea wandered through the cluster of booths that formed an outer ring around the Sacred Circle. With a little luck, she'd run across Four Bears or one of the other Dakota tribesmen.

Instead, she found Ann leaning over a table of silver and turquoise jewelry. Cullen stood next to her, staring into the milling crowd. His mind seemed to be a million miles away. She thought he'd be more alert considering the attack on him and Ethan's murder.

He spied her through the crowd and motioned her toward them.

"Shea, dear. So glad you could come."

Besides the white satin sling, he wore a pearl-gray suit and white patent leather loafers. Did the man not own casual wear? She wondered if he slept in a suit. She'd have to ask Ann.

While she was at it, she'd remind her friend of the pact they'd made to stay away from Blade and Cullen until everything was settled. She couldn't scold Ann too much, considering she agreed to meet with Blade later.

Ann popped up from her scrutiny of the jewelry and flashed Shea a smile that rivaled her bright orange and yellow squaw dress. A matching cloth squash blossom held her blonde hair back from her face.

"Come look at the fabulous pair of earrings I found," Ann said.

Joining them, Shea agreed the turquoise and coral studded ear posts were smashing. Ann opened a drawstring cloth purse that matched her dress material and drew out a twenty dollar bill.

Cullen stepped away to examine a nearby bow and quiver. As soon as the bauble was paid for, he returned.

What a jerk.

Ann turned to Shea and gushed with excitement. "We have good news."

"I could use some good news."

"The lieutenant insisted that Tom Bennett check the entire display of Indian artifacts restored by Blade and his men. So far, they're all authentic. Restored, but the real thing."

"Then how does Blade explain the fake?"

Shea prayed he had a satisfactory explanation. Could that be what he wanted to tell her?

Ann donned first one earring, then the other. "Oh, Cheek and Blade figured that out. Cheek said he didn't know why he hadn't thought of it before. He'd asked Blade to make a few duplicates for the museum's teaching room, where we hold hands-on seminars for school children. Cheek hadn't realized Blade already started on the reproductions. Somehow, the replica lance got mixed in with the restored pieces. The real lance went to the teaching room. An honest mistake."

Cullen snorted.

"You don't believe them?" Shea asked.

"I believe that's the excuse Blade gave Cheek. And Cheek, in his enthusiasm for this whole mess to be done with, accepted his word on the matter. You know how these Indians are. They don't sign contracts if they can help it. Their word is their bond." He said the last in a sarcastic mimic.

"I can't say I blame Cheek," Ann said. "I'm glad the forgery issue is over."

"As am I," Cullen agreed.

Shea wasn't satisfied. "Were there other replicas in the teaching room?"

"A ceremonial clay pipe and a buffalo-hide shield," Ann said.

Shea remembered when Blade and Cheek brought a shield to

the storeroom. She'd wondered why the men seemed unenthused about the relic. Had it been the real one or a fake? She recalled Four Bears cleaning the shield at the workshop.

"Mistakenly, Billy took the duplicate lance to Ethan," Ann explained. "The authentic lance must have been delivered to the teaching room. In the excitement, it was forgotten. Everything's straightened out now."

Shea couldn't believe her ears. "Everything except Ethan's murder."

"Of course, I didn't mean to imply—"

Cullen cut in. "With the forgery issue cleared up, it's apparent his death was just a senseless robbery attempt after all."

"Poor Ethan," Ann said, sadness creeping into her voice. "He must have planned to take the fake lance home until it could be verified. You know how obstinate he was, bless his heart. Not knowing who to trust, he thought he was doing the right thing."

Shea would not let them sweep this aside. "What about the attempt on Cullen's life?"

The director shook his head. "Maybe one of Blade's men thought I was going to bring charges of forgery against him and struck out at me. With that settled amicably and their chief no longer a suspect, they'll be returning to the reservation tomorrow. And I'll no longer be in danger. I've informed Lieutenant Jansen that I don't wish to pursue the matter."

"Then Jansen is satisfied we're all not killers?"

Cullen shrugged. "He says if we're comfortable with the explanation of how the fake lance came to be passed off as a relic, he'll accept that. But he still has a murder to solve. Only now the suspect list includes every known felon in St. Louis, so he's not very happy."

Shea wasn't very happy either. As pat as the explanation sounded, she wondered how Blade could've forgotten they'd made a substitute. They'd already made a duplicate clay pipe and shield.

She glanced at Ann, no longer a murder suspect, who appeared happy with the decision. The museum wouldn't have to deal with forged artifacts. Cullen was out of danger. And Blade was off the hook, too. Shea should be able to muster some pleasure with all that.

Still, she couldn't shake the feeling something was wrong. She remembered how both Ethan and Tom Bennett could *feel* that the war lance wasn't authentic. The heft of it. Its smell. Then why couldn't Blade, an expert restorer? As far as Shea was concerned, this whole thing reeked.

"So come Monday, things will be back to normal at the museum," she stated without conviction.

"Mostly," Ann said. "But I've decided it would be prudent to check the catalog sheets against the relics in the gallery to make sure the inventory is correct."

Cullen went rigid. "What?"

"I'm going to inventory the relics," Ann repeated.

He grabbed her arm. She flinched, a startled look on her face.

"An excellent idea," he said. "I don't know why I didn't think of it." He turned to Shea. "Please excuse us. We have to go."

He left her standing alone as he dragged a stunned Ann toward the parked cars.

Twenty-Seven

Shea resumed her search for Blade and his men. She wanted to believe Cullen and Ann, that it was all a misunderstanding. Ethan's death was simply a mugging gone wrong. That he planned to take the lance home for safekeeping until it was authenticated, but he met with disaster.

Something didn't make sense. She found it difficult to believe Cullen dismissed his wounding so readily. And Ann, who'd bought a handgun to protect them, seemed to accept his decision without argument.

Scanning the milling crowd, Shea didn't see how she'd find Blade's men. Indians surrounded her—talking, laughing, dressed in tribal costume or full regalia. Some with red or blond hair didn't look as if they had a drop of Indian blood in them. DNA could be a trickster; burying certain traits, accentuating others. She'd seen people who looked like twins, and they weren't even related. On the other hand, one short family member with straight black hair might share the same genes with a tall, blond, curly headed sibling. Go figure.

Passing a booth filled with knives, sheaths, and arrowheads, she paused and picked up a bone-handle knife similar to the Arikara one that nearly dispatched Cullen. Its blade shone sharp and lethal in the light from a nearby lantern.

Someone touched Shea's arm. "Excuse me."

Startled, she spun around, the knife still clutched in her hand.

Tom Bennett jumped backwards out of reach.

"I'm sorry. I didn't mean to frighten you." She placed the weapon back onto the table.

"Other than a few years shaved from my life span, no harm done." He peered at her through horn-rimmed bifocals. "I thought I recognized you from the museum."

"Yes, but we were never introduced." She stuck out her hand. "My name's Shea McKenna, Mr. Bennett. I'm photographing the relics for the museum."

He smiled and shook her hand. "Please, call me Tom. I saw the patron's books. Nice job."

"Thanks."

As friendly as Bennett seemed, she wasn't sure where he fit into the scheme of things. Was he friend or foe?

"Ann tells me they've found the real lance, the one that was duplicated," she said, feeling him out. "In the children's showroom."

A frown replaced his smile. "Yes, that's true."

"Then you examined it?"

"Yes, yes." His eyebrows knitted in puzzlement.

"Is everything all right?"

"What? Oh, yes. Under the circumstances, I gave it a thorough going over. It's the real thing. Restored, of course, but the real thing. I place it in the mid 1800s."

"Then what's wrong?"

He moved closer. "You say you're photographing the relics? Then you understand."

What did he mean? She understood Ethan was dead, Cullen had been attacked, and no one seemed to know what was going on. She'd never get anything out of Bennett, however, with that answer.

Fake it, girl.

"Yes, I know what happened, but I find it strange no one remembered duplicates of certain artifacts were made for the children's showroom."

"That's a puzzler, isn't it?" He stroked his chin. "You'd think they would've been more thorough before calling me in from Santa Fe again."

"Ethan's death has everyone on edge. Clear thinking seems to be at a premium."

Blade was no fool, nor easily rattled. He may not have known where the real lance disappeared to, but he had to have known a duplicate was made. Maybe that's what Bennett meant. Blade had seen and held the fake lance. As an Indian, he would know if it was real or not. As an artist, he'd recognize his own work. Once again, the ball was back in Blade's court.

And the attempt on Cullen's life still needed to be reckoned with. Maybe now that everyone seemed satisfied, Blade would set her mind at ease about his role in this mess. She needed to find the Dakota chieftain. This time, she wouldn't let him slip away without answering her questions.

"Have you seen Blade?" she asked Bennett with as much indifference as she could muster. If the relic expert was involved, she didn't want to scare him into silence.

He shook his head. "No, sorry."

"I suppose you're old acquaintances. Both of you working with relics. And both of you from Santa Fe."

"I've been to his studio. He does magnificent work. In fact, I recommended him to Cheek."

If Lieutenant Jansen was still tracking down forgers, he'd consider Blade and Bennett possible cohorts. She needed to coax more information from Bennett. "Then you were surprised to hear allegations of a forgery?"

"Surprised? I'm shocked. Blade's an outstanding artist and a chief's son. To jeopardize his career and standing with the tribe, he'd have to have an awfully compelling reason."

"You don't think making thousands of dollars selling Indian artifacts to the European market or to private collectors here in the United States is sufficient reason?"

"Not for Blade. He's devoted to his people. He'd never do anything to embarrass or harm them."

"Is he devoted enough to do anything to build a clinic?"

Bennett stared at her in silence for a moment, then answered, "I see your point. I don't like it, but I see your point."

Twenty-Eight

Leaving Tom Bennett to mull over her words, Shea resumed her search for Blade. Before she got very far, she spied Gram, Aunt Kathryn, Professor Wakefield, and Philip Ross coming toward her. They appeared to be dressed for another night at a ball. The men wore suits, and Kathryn had tucked herself into a floor-length red taffeta evening gown. Gram wore her usual lace and pearls.

"Let me get a picture of this," Shea teased as she squinted into her camera's viewfinder. "Gram, where're your moccasins?"

Gram waved a flowered hanky at her. "Oh, pish-posh. We're going to another charity function. We dropped by for a few minutes to meet your Indian friends. I didn't get to at the Ball."

"I was just looking for them." She kissed Gram and nodded at the others. "Hello Jonathan. Kathryn. Philip. It seems like only yesterday—"

"Can it," Kathryn said. "Where's—" She glanced in Philip's direction. "Anything special we should see?"

Shea got the hint. "I was just about to take a few shots of the dancers. Want to join me, Katie?"

"I'd love to." Kathryn grabbed hold of Shea's elbow and pushed her toward the Sacred Circle, leaving the others behind. "Why do you insist on calling me that name? You know you're the only one I allow to do that and let live."

"I appreciate the gesture."

"Don't be long, Kathryn," Gram requested, waving her hanky after them. "We have to be at the Athletic Club soon."

Shea pulled her arm lose from Kathryn's grasp. "Athletic Club? The four of you gonna run a few laps? Pump iron?"

She pointed the Nikon at a cluster of Dog Soldiers, recognizable by their cloth sashes, warrior's stance, and black and white painted faces. They gathered at the entrance to the Sacred Circle.

"The club's holding a benefit dinner. For survivors of Hurricane Katrina who've resettled in St. Louis."

"Worthy cause. Make a donation for me. I'll pay you back later."

Her attention shifted as she lowered the camera and stared at the Dog Soldiers. One of them had stepped aside to reveal Blade in their midst. They moved away from the others as their conversation grew more animated. She recognized the man's split facial markings—black on top, white on bottom—as that of the Indian she'd bumped into earlier.

"What's wrong?" Kathryn asked.

Blade and the man's gestures grew more intense, ending with the Dog Soldier making a universal sign understood in any language—a slashing across the throat with his hand. After which, he strode away.

Kathryn nudged her. "Shea?"

"What? Oh, nothing's wrong. There," Shea pointed at Blade, "is the object of my screwed up intentions."

"Translates well from tux to buckskin."

"Yes," Shea breathed. "Yes, he does."

Neither one spoke as they continued to gape at the handsome chieftain. At how his biceps bulged beneath the long sleeves of his tight-fitting chief's shirt. How his waist tapered from firm abs to trim hips and taut thighs. How he stood with legs spread and arms folded across his broad chest like some great ancient warrior. Eventually, she felt her aunt's attention shift as Kathryn leaned closer.

"Be careful, Shea. Don't make a mistake here."

"I know."

Kathryn shook her head. "I don't think you do."

Shea turned and stared into Kathryn's hooded eyes. Gone was the playful sparkle, replaced by a sincerity that bore through her. "If you think this man could be the one, take the time and effort to find out for sure. Don't let your work or travels or your fear of commitment get in the way. You may regret it for the rest of your life." She paused, then said, "I know I do."

Shea sucked in the woodsy park air, the smoke from the council fire, the cloying scent of body heat. It left her light-headed. "Nothing's forever," she whispered. "Just ask my mother."

"Nobody promised you it would be."

"Once we were a happy family. Now Mom's in her grave. And Dad's living in D. C. where I seldom get to see him."

"And you're hopping from here to there all over the world, running scared."

Shea lowered her tone a notch. "I hope you can tread water, Katie, 'cause you're skating on thin ice."

Kathryn ignored the threat, taking hold of Shea's arm again. "I especially regret not having kids. Or a husband."

Shea sloughed off her aunt's hand. "I don't want to hear this." She refused to believe her life, her firm foundation, was made of kindling—nor would she tolerate Kathryn setting a match to it.

"I see the way you look at him," Kathryn persisted. "Now and at the Ball last night. How you clung to him while you danced on the terrace."

Had the whole world spied on them? First Ann confessed, now Kathryn.

"I won't listen to this any more."

She kept moving, head down, away from her aunt's scrutiny, away from the probing questions, away from the hurtful words. When she raised her eyes again, she found it difficult to see. Wiping away tears, she stood once again at the Sacred Circle.

Blade was no longer there.

Twenty-Nine

Fearing Blade might return to the Circle and catch her crying, Shea hurried toward a small group of Indian women and children.

Philip Ross cut her off. She swiped at her eyes.

"Are you alright?" He touched her arm.

"I'm-I'm fine." She brushed again at her damp cheeks, stumbling over the lie. "The smoke from the bonfire…"

She couldn't deal with Philip. Not now. Not tactfully, anyway. Too many things ran through her mind. Gnawing at her insides. What remained after Kathryn thoroughly ripped them out.

She cast around for a way to escape without hurting Philip's feelings. "Where's the rest of your entourage?" she asked.

Jonathan, Kathryn, and Gram were nowhere in sight. It wouldn't do for Gram to see her crying. The old softie would badger her the rest of the night in an effort to dispel whatever brought tears to her granddaughter's eyes.

"I wanted to see you again," Philip said. "Before you left for Mexico."

"Aren't you afraid you'll miss your ride to the charity dinner?"

"Your grandmother walks slowly. I can catch up with them." He paused. "Or I could stay here. I've never seen a powwow."

No!

Blade wanted to talk to her. It's what she'd been waiting for. An explanation for his strange behavior. For the forged relic. For Ethan's murder. He won't come if he sees Philip.

"You're welcome to stay," she said, "but I have work to do. I'll be moving around a lot. Taking pictures for a layout for...uh."

Rats! What was the story she'd cooked up? Oh, yeah.

"For *Anthropology Today.*"

He stuffed his hands in his pockets and looked away.

Was she that transparent?

He turned back.

"Look, Shea, we got off to a bad start. I stalled when Jonathan asked me to take you out as a favor. Your grandmother had been needling him to fix us up on a date."

Well, that was sure flattering.

"I balked. I've had bad experiences with blind dates. One of them is still stalking me." He smiled to show he was joking—maybe. "When I finally agreed to meet you, I couldn't believe my good luck." Ducking his head, he toed the ground between them. "You're beautiful. And smart."

Okay, this was getting better. She no longer felt like a bucked-tooth, cross-eyed, mail-order bride. Her resolve to keep him at arms' length softened.

"I was at a loss for words," he continued. "It was like you cast a spell over me. I guess I came off pretty lame."

He did have nice eyes. And dimples when he smiled. Come to think of it, he bore a strong resemblance to her perfect man, the long-deceased archeologist Richard Halliburton.

She offered an encouraging smile.

He cupped her hand in his, running his thumb lightly over her wrist. "Anyway, maybe we could try again. Looks like we'll be working together in Mexico."

Kathryn's words nagged at her. *Be careful, Shea. Don't make a mistake. If this man could be the one...*

But which man? Blade or Philip? Or did another man wait somewhere in the future? Was she in danger of choosing too soon?

She removed her hand from his. "Then we'll see each other in Mexico."

He smiled, but there was no joy in his words. "Then Mexico, it is."

Thirty

More confused about her feelings than ever, Shea moved on to the cluster of Indian women and children. Three stunningly attired females preened over a young boy who looked no older than eight or nine years.

Her calm somewhat restored, Shea complimented one of the women. "That's a lovely outfit. Do you mind if I take your picture?"

The young woman gazed at her with soft doe eyes. She wore a wine-colored brushed buckskin dress. Long buckskin fringe swayed at the hem and shoulders. Small brown and white shells, polished to a sheen, covered her bodice. Matching knee-high moccasins shod her tiny feet.

"This is my wedding dress," she said shyly, fiddling with one of her long braids. "My fiancé made it for me."

She pointed to a tall brave standing beside a group of men waiting for the next dance.

The whole world finds love except Kathryn and me. Did I make the right choice to follow in her footsteps?

Shea tried to dismiss the agonizing thoughts and concentrate on the women and their young charge. The shell bracelet she wore matched the shells on the young bride-to-be's dress. She had bought the piece of jewelry in Tahiti.

"Here." She slid it off her wrist. "A wedding present. It matches your dress."

The young woman timidly bowed her head. "Oh, thank you. We're to be married next month at sunrise. At Cahokia Mounds. You can come, if you like."

"If I'm back in town, I'd love to. Could I take pictures of your wedding? Maybe *Historic Cultures* magazine will run them."

One of the other women inched up to Shea. "Her name is Morning Star," the short plump newcomer said. "She's Sioux. She's my best friend. My name is Summer Rain. I'm Sioux and Fox. And that's Tara Gray Dove."

She pointed to the woman dressed in a satiny turquoise dress with white fringe and white moccasins standing next to the boy. "She's Cherokee."

"You ladies are so beautiful. What lovely names." Shea snapped their pictures. "I'm plain old Shea."

Star giggled and handed Rain her feather fan to hold while she searched through a rawhide pouch. She brought out a small box. Inside, a single feather and bead strung on a thin strip of leather lay on a bed of cotton. She took it out and tied it around Shea's neck.

"I made this," Star said.

Shea was touched by her friendliness. "Thank you. But why—"

"Because you gave a gift to me. It is custom that I reciprocate. And because I can tell you have the heart of an Indian. Your name will no longer be 'plain old Shea,'" she said with an air of solemnity, "but 'Woman With Heart of Indian.'"

It wasn't enough to have the heart of an Indian—did she possess Blade's heart?—she needed the form of an Indian to be suitable for him. He was a chieftain. His tribe would expect him to marry an Indian woman.

Philip liked her as she was.

Shea thanked Star again and turned toward the young boy so the woman couldn't hear the catch in her voice. "What's your name?"

Tara Gray Dove spoke for the boy who, Shea learned, was her son. "His name is Jason Gray Dove."

"I'm nine years old," he said as if he considered himself no longer a child—at least for today.

"He will someday be a chief," Rain said.

Dressed differently than the other children, the little boy was decked out in a red and yellow chief's shirt, white leggings, and a black buckskin breechcloth. Red satin ribbons dangled from his shirt yoke. But his feathers were the major difference. A headdress of five large turkey feathers and a turkey feather bustle tipped in red seemed as if it would weigh down such a small body. He stood tall and straight, however, and bore a solemn, almost regal, expression befitting a future chief. Was this how Blade looked as a child?

Would Shea someday have children of her own? Or would she regret the loss of their love as Kathryn did?

Reminded of Blade, she took the young chieftain's picture and moved on. She arrived back at the Sacred Circle in time for a new dance. Billy Quintella stood at the circle's entrance with Four Bears.

She nodded a greeting.

Four Bears wore full coyote regalia like the Indian she nearly collided with by the tepee. At the time, she thought he looked vaguely familiar. He also wore a knife sheathed to his waist and another tucked down in his knee-high moccasins. He'd painted the right side of his face white; the left side black. Was Four Bears demonstrating conflicting feelings about restoring relics for the museum?

"Humph," he grunted in response to her greeting, but refused to look at her. Even a compliment on his outfit failed to dent his granite exterior.

She peeked around him at Billy. "We meet again."

The young Indian answered her with a wide grin. Four Bears frowned. Not wanting to get Billy in trouble, she directed her questions at the big Indian.

"Where are Elk Horn and Blade?"

She tried to act equally interested in the whereabouts of both men but hadn't fooled Four Bears.

"Blade's in the wickiup, the sweat lodge, with the local chief and tribal leaders."

He let her know from his tone she was lucky he bothered to talk to her.

"They smoke the Sacred Pipe. When they are through, he will dance in the Sacred Circle." He shot her a piercing stare. "Don't bother him."

"Of course not," she said as if it were the furthest thing from her mind. "I understand Blade is an important man among the Sioux."

"Do you understand *how* important. Blade's father is a good chief. But he is old, with old ways. He fears protesting injustices will bring retaliation. If not from the government, then from white people who hate us for no reason.

"Blade has plans for the tribe," he said with pride. "To bring us into the twenty-first century. The clinic is just the beginning. He will go to Washington. Lobby the government for what's rightfully ours, what the white man takes for granted. Good paying jobs off the reservation. A college education for our sons and daughters. And someday, freedom from prejudice and oppression. Blade will do this," Four Bears added. "And he'll raise his sons—his Indian sons—to carry on our fight for justice."

"I understand," Shea responded in a whisper.

"Do you understand?"

"Yes," she repeated more vehemently. "I understand."

"Too bad Jansen doesn't. Charging Blade—our future chief—with murder would embarrass the tribe, weakening Blade's power."

Hadn't the Indians been informed their chieftain was no longer a prime suspect in Ethan's murder? At the group interrogation, the lieutenant made it clear everyone was a suspect, with Blade at the top of his list. But now that the matter of the fake lance was cleared up, they were equally suspect. Somehow that thought didn't help.

"When it comes to murder," Shea said, "I'm afraid Lieutenant Jansen sees it as his duty to suspect everyone."

"Only a coward would kill a frail old man. The Sioux wouldn't choose a coward to lead them."

"I'm sure you're right."

In her heart, she felt the same way. Logically, she wasn't so sure. She couldn't believe Cheek's lame explanation about the fake lance would satisfy Jansen. Maybe Blade had considered Ethan a threat to the tribe's welfare, an enemy that needed to be eliminated.

Again the terrible question raised its ugly head. Was Blade guilty? And was Cheek his accomplice? If Cullen spent the night with Ann, as she claims, then Cheek has no alibi. Together, Blade and Cheek could've planned to deceive the museum, and either one of them could've killed Ethan.

And Cullen.

Was Ann in danger?

Am I?

Shea eyed Four Bears. "Where were you the night Ethan died?"

"Helping my chief," he said and walked away.

Helping Blade with the relics or helping him kill Ethan? Straightforward questions didn't seem to be getting her anywhere. She'd try subtlety.

She sidled up to Billy, but before she could quiz him, action in the Sacred Circle drew their attention.

Thirty-One

"Look," Billy called to Shea. "They're about to start a Blanket Dance."

An Indian woman dressed in an ankle-length white skirt trimmed in red and blue laid a blanket in front of the large drum in the middle of the Sacred Circle. The loudspeaker crackled with static as a voice announced this dance would be in honor of the medical clinic to be built on the Dakota reservation. More beaters with smaller drums joined the chanter. The cadence of their drumming slowed so all the people could participate.

Men, women, and children entered the circle. This time they added a shuffle to their toe-heel step. Besides their feather fans and rattles, they clutched something undetectable in their hands.

"What happens in a Blanket Dance?" Shea asked Billy.

"Watch."

When the dancers rounded the drum and came to the blanket, they each threw what they clutched onto it. Coins bounced and paper money fluttered in the breeze.

"They're throwing money," Shea said with wonder.

Billy nodded. "For the clinic. Although the museum's contributing, it's not enough. We'll need supplies and doctors and nurses. There are few jobs on the reservation and little money. The Indian Nation helps each other. From all over the United States and Canada they come."

He paused and watched the dancers, young and old, contribute, their heads held high.

"A long time ago the government outlawed giveaways among our people," he said. "They tried to erase our old ways so we wouldn't have each other to depend on and could be easily assimilated into the rest of society. To kill our spirit." Billy's tone turned dark. "They even punished our children in school if they spoke their native tongue. But we hid our ways. Practiced them secretly. It's useless for the government to try to stop the old ways. From council fire to council fire, we hand down the traditions of our people to the next generation."

Although she sympathized with what he said, the passion and anger in Billy's voice stunned Shea. Aroused for the right cause, could he kill a man? It was Billy who brought the wrong lance to Ethan. Had he purposely started this whole confrontation in an effort to compel his people to take a stand?

"Blade practices the old ways?" she asked, still wondering if Billy was devious enough to force his chieftain's hand.

"Blade lives in both worlds. He doesn't always stay on the reservation, but his heart is there. He's a good chieftain. What the Indian sings about, Blade paints, so the world will know and understand."

The drumming stopped. The dancers left the circle. A hush fell over the crowd as the announcer spoke again.

"This is a special dance by the men who've been praying in the wickiup for the clinic," Billy whispered with respect.

The crowd parted and a path formed leading to a domed structure made of canvas and blankets. The front flap thrown aside, steam drifted out. A lone figure stepped through the opening.

Blade Santee.

Shea's heart jolted at the sight of him.

He wore a buckskin breechcloth and fringed leggings. An eagle feather headdress fluttered down his sweat-glistened back to his feet. Gone were the Gucci loafers; in their place, beaded moccasins. Head held high and back straight, he strode toward the Sacred Circle.

A red and white choker and breastplate made of long bone

beads known as "hair pipes" rattled as he walked. His muscular arms and firm coppery buttocks shone in the light of the council fire. A tantalizing heat burned inside Shea at the sight of the nearly naked Dakota chieftain.

Four more men, who displayed the bearing of chiefs, marched behind him. As they passed her and entered the circle, she noticed Blade appeared to be in a trance, set apart from the people around him. With a twinge of disappointment, she realized he hadn't seen her.

He began to move to the beat of the drum. He dipped and leaped. He spun in circles around, around, and around the blazing bonfire, his long black hair flying wildly about him. The fire's red flames seemed to draw him closer. The other chiefs followed, but stayed apart.

The singer's chanting hit a vibrant crescendo. The drums thundered. The council fire crackled and spit sparks into the night air.

A lump rose in Shea's throat as Blade twisted and stamped and twirled toward her. His powerful body gleamed with sweat; muscles stretched tight, his eyes ablaze. Something raw and primordial tore at her heart.

Turning, he came face to face with her, but his eyes focused on something far away; another place, another time, before the white man, when the land and the sky and the waters were unpolluted, when the buffalo ranged plentiful, and the Indian answered to no man.

Raising high a war lance similar to the one used to kill Ethan, Blade spun in a frenzied circle in front of her. She felt as if she were being sucked into the vortex of his gyrating dance, pulled into his anger, rage, and sorrow. His spirit seemed to reach out to her, touching her, searching. She gasped for air, the billowing smoke of the council fire burning her lungs.

Eyes closed, he halted in front of her.

The drums stopped.

He stood quietly for a moment, his breath escaping in short, ragged gasps. When he opened his eyes again, they focused on Shea.

Thirty-Two

Blade leapt over the ring of serape-covered benches and strode toward Shea. His hair-pipe breastplate rattled eerily. The eagle feather headdress rustled as it fanned out behind him. Backlit by the glowing council fire, he looked and sounded like some mythical creature—half eagle, half man. Both predatory.

Shea's breath caught, then escaped in a whimper when he halted before her. She didn't know whether to run or submit.

"Hormones," she whispered. "Hormones."

His gaze raked over her, from her awestruck eyes to her quivering mouth to her heaving breasts straining against the pearl snaps on her blouse. As they stared at each other, the drums began again their haunting rhythm.

"I'm glad you waited for me," he said, perspiration beading his forehead.

She took a deep breath. His scent of leather and testosterone made her giddy. As much as she wanted to, it wouldn't do for her to allow Blade to throw her to the ground and make mad, passionate love to her in the middle of a powwow. Someone had to show a little restraint.

"I'm glad too," she said.

He'd already told her he planned to leave tomorrow for the reservation. The thought of never seeing him again left an empty feeling in the pit of her stomach.

"There's something I must tell you," he said.

"I know. The relics are genuine—and the duplicates are for

the classroom." She couldn't hide her skepticism.

"There's more." He gently clasped her hand and led her to the forest at the edge of the powwow—away from prying eyes.

A bittersweet dread filled her.

"I should've been honest with you from the beginning. But then Ethan was murdered, and Cullen attacked... I didn't know what to say without causing more trouble. Without more bloodshed. This is all my fault."

No. No, no, no. He was admitting to murder. Until he actually said it, she'd hoped he was innocent. Needed him to be innocent. Wanted passionately for him to be innocent.

"You should know the truth before I go," he said. "So you won't think so badly of me."

She looked back at the Sacred Circle. Like the dancers, her mind spun dizzily. The word "murderer" pounded in her ears, in tempo with the thundering drums. Her knees weakened and she leaned against a large oak.

He reached for her.

Sick with the knowledge of his guilt, she waved his hand away.

"Please," he said, "wait here until I return this headdress to the tribal leaders. Then we'll talk. I promise you the truth."

Unable to speak, she closed her eyes and nodded. When she opened them again, he was gone. She sucked in another deep breath and braced herself for his return—and what he planned to tell her.

A hissing sound followed by a heavy thud startled her. Instinctively, she ducked. What was going on? She stared in shock at the Bowie knife embedded in the tree above her. It quivered with the force of the impact. Light from a nearby booth danced along its lethal blade.

Her eyes searched the milling crowd. Indians and spectators roamed about, buying merchandise, watching dancers, eating fry bread. No one seemed aware of what happened.

Slowly, she rose and watched for a sign of her attacker. No one looked her way, caught her eye.

She glanced again at the knife only inches from her face. If she hadn't leaned against the tree...

Alert now, her mind raced as her eyes sifted the crowd. One of those innocent-looking people just tried to kill her. She wanted to run but had no idea which way to go, whom to avoid, whom to trust.

Blade, tempting her with the promise of information, brought her to the edge of the woods. Told her to stay there.

Had he set her up? Maybe he or one of his men decided to get rid of the white woman who asked too many questions.

Scrambling behind the huge oak, she scanned the crowd again and groaned in frustration. Lieutenant Jansen had promised to be at the powwow.

Where's the cavalry when you need it?

For all she knew, they could be disguised as Indians. But which one?

She spied Billy laughing with a group of young braves. For the first time that night, she saw Elk Horn inspecting a knife sheath at a nearby craft booth. Had there been a knife in the scabbard? Cheek's threat in the museum storeroom left little doubt what he'd do if he caught her alone. Was that what he was demonstrating to Blade when she saw them with the Dog Soldiers?

She continued to search for help. Tom Bennett was nowhere in sight. Cullen and Ann had left. So had Philip and her family.

Summer Rain and Morning Star conversed now with Four Bears at the entrance to the Sacred Circle. Were the women angry because Blade showered her with too much attention? The handsome chieftain was quite a catch. Four Bears warned her it wouldn't sit well with his tribe if Blade became involved with a white woman. The big Indian could have thrown the knife tucked in his knee-high moccasins or the one in his belt. Would the women alibi him, one of their own, or defend someone they'd just met?

Shea grabbed at the knife to arm herself. Her hands slipped. She wiped damp palms on her jeans and tried again, but she couldn't dislodge the embedded weapon.

She spied Blade moving toward her through the crowd, his face intent as if he were about to confess to murder. Or commit one. Was he coming to finish the job?

Panic set in. Fear gripped her. She was on her own. No one would come to her rescue. Screaming or trying to lose herself in a crowd of strangers would be too dangerous. Before she raised an alarm, someone could shove a blade between her ribs.

She'd have to escape them all.

Her apartment lay on the other side of the forest across Skinker Boulevard. Maybe someone on the street would help her. A jogger. Someone in a passing car. Until then, her only hope would be to outrun her assailant.

She glanced behind her at the crowd one last time. Blade struggled toward her through the throng. Elk Horn had disappeared. Four Bears turned and looked in her direction. A puzzled frown creased his black and white painted features. Was he surprised to see her still alive?

She didn't wait to find out. Securing her camera against her body, she plunged into the dense woods.

No stranger to frantic flight, she'd often gotten herself into tight situations when photographing wild animals. If it hadn't been for a Maasai gun bearer on a trek across the Serengeti for *National Geographic*, she'd have ended up as a hungry lion's tasty meal. The Maasai frightened the big cat away, and she learned a valuable lesson. Don't back a dangerous animal into a corner.

That's exactly what she'd done. She'd showed up at the powwow asking questions. An explanation, however unreasonable it sounded, had already been offered. But she wasn't a reasonable person, not when it came to murder.

Someone crashed into the woods behind her.

She increased her speed. Her heart thumped wildly, mimicking the primitive thud of the council drum that boomed louder and louder. She ran in rhythm to its beat. Faster. Faster. Faster.

Her breathing grew ragged, uneven, stressed. She gulped in the fresh, damp air, tasting the air-borne spores of moldy leaves and rotting wood that carpeted the forest floor. Low hanging branches slapped against her face and arms and inflicted stinging welts. Their domain disturbed, angry gnats and mosquitoes swarmed around her head. With her free hand, she shielded her eyes, but the action provided little protection and blocked her view. The woods seemed to go on forever.

The thrashing behind her came closer. Every shadow, every noise sent an electric shock along her spine, spurring her on. Her own imagination was her worse enemy. Indians in war paint and battle regalia lurked behind every tree, crouched with raised weapons behind every bush, waited for her beyond the bend.

Fear propelled her forward. Her heart caught in her throat when she envisioned what he would do to her with the knife. Stumbling over a tree root, she plunged headlong into darkness, striking her head on a large stone.

She lay there a moment, dazed and gasping for air. She hated scenes when actresses in scary movies slipped and fell. The cliché made the heroine look clumsy and stupid. That's how Shea felt, clumsy and stupid. And in pain. Swiping at a trickle of wetness on her forehead, her hand came away dark and sticky. She lay back a second to collect her wits.

Above the beating of the drums and the painful throbbing in her head, she heard her pursuer moving swiftly. She didn't have time to plan a calm, intelligent defense. It was flight or fight. No way was she ready to take on a cold-blooded killer, but the adrenaline fear produced suddenly evaporated.

Gasping for air, she stood. She had to keep going. A wave of nausea swept over her, and she fell to the ground again. Head spinning, she lay there and listened. Whoever was chasing her had stopped. No, wait, she heard a rustle of leaves, a twig snap, another, then nothing.

Whoever it was must have paused to reconnoiter. He waited now for her to move. To make a sound.

Holding her breath, she peered through the inky tangle of vines and saplings, past the massive oaks and elms that stood before Missouri was inhabited by anyone other than the Indian. She was on their ground, a hundred years before the coming of the white man. They had the advantage.

She looked in the direction she'd been running. A dim light glowed beyond the forest.

Streetlights!

Home and safety lay within reach. The possibility bolstered her with new-found energy. She rose and raced headlong toward the light. Ignoring the noise she made and her aching head, she concentrated on reaching her apartment. Her heart felt like it was going to burst as she stumbled onto a path leading out of the woods. She whispered a prayer of thanks and raced along it.

But her pursuer stayed with her. She could hear the pounding of his feet on the forest floor. The breaking of twigs and rustling of leaves. Of branches slapping against his body, as they'd done hers. She wondered if the welts they inflicted stung him as badly. Or was he immune to pain, his mind occupied with thoughts of killing her.

She neared the forest's edge now. The streetlights glowed brighter. A car zipped past, then nothing. A stabbing pain shot through her side. Tired and hurting, she couldn't last much longer. Her legs ached, her head throbbed, but hope spurred her on. With every ounce of willpower she possessed, she increased her speed.

The runner was nearly upon her. His labored breathing echoed in her ears. Was it Elk Horn? Four Bears? She was afraid to turn and look, afraid it would cause her to lose ground.

Was it Blade?

Oh, god, don't let it be Blade.

As her feet pounded along the path, the camera hanging around her neck bounced painfully against her chest. She'd let go of it when she fell. Discarding it crossed her mind, but her Scottish ancestry wouldn't let her pitch the expensive equipment into the weeds. Funny how instinct and upbringing influenced you, even at the most inconvenient times. She wished there'd been more long distance runners than Kathryn in her bloodline. Right now she needed all the genetic help she could get.

Lifting the camera away from her body to alleviate the pain, she was struck with an idea. She stopped and spun around to face her assailant before she lost her nerve. The camera was set on auto focus. She aimed and pressed the Nikon's shutter release.

The button clicked. The flash lighted up a fifteen-foot circle, blinding her pursuer in the ring of light. He threw his arms across his face, but it was too late.

In that bright, blazing instant, Shea clearly saw who chased her.

Thirty-Three

Blinded by the camera's flash, the Dog Soldier staggered and flailed the night air with a large Bowie knife. His black and white painted face contorted as he screamed with rage.

Shea stared in horror, his image burned in her brain. It was Four Bears.

Oh, no. No

Was Blade his accomplice?

No!

Please. No.

She wanted to sink to her knees, to give up. She was so tired. And she hurt. They'd brutally murdered Ethan. And now they planned to kill her.

Sorrow engulfed her. Then fear as Four Bears staggered forward. He swung the lethal knife dangerously close to her face. The light from a street lamp glinted off its blade.

He must've pulled it from the tree before he came after her. If it was the same knife. He always wore one at his waist and another tucked in his knee-high moccasins. She dare not let her eyes stray from his to check.

He swung the knife at her again. And again, he missed. As soon as he regained his sight, it would all be over. She had to act now.

Gathering what little strength still left, she turned and raced for her apartment across the deserted boulevard. Not a car was in sight. No lights were on in her grandmother's house. They must still be at the charity dinner. Maybe a neighbor—

"Help. Help me!" she shouted.

Windows closed and air conditioners running full blast to ward off the July heat, no one heard her screams. Or if they had, didn't want to get involved. A woman was raped and murdered on the park's running path last year. No witnesses came forward.

Shea raced across the avenue's wide expanse, praying to stay ahead of her attacker. She willed herself not to look behind. What difference did it make how close he was? If he caught her, she was dead. Dead was dead.

He must have regained his sight. She could hear his footfalls. Closer. Coming closer. If she lived, the sound would haunt her for the rest of her life.

Breathless, she ducked into the alley behind Gram's house that ran perpendicular to Skinker. The old cobblestone roadway was uneven and treacherous in the dark. Staggering on a loose stone, she slammed into a brick wall.

The jarring collision knocked her to the ground. Gasping for air, she clung to the structure and pulled herself up. Where was he? She could hear movement, a soft padding like moccasins moving fast along the dark alley.

With every ounce of strength she could muster, Shea pushed away from the wall. She found it wasn't a building she'd collided with, but the brick-enclosed courtyard of the house next to Gram's.

An electric charge of hope shot through her. She stumbled along in the darkness toward her carriage house beyond the courtyard. Heavy footfalls echoed behind her. Her legs felt as if they would give out.

Rounding the corner of the wall, she spied the white wrought-iron stairs leading to her apartment. But her strength was depleted. She wouldn't make it. She struggled forward. Stopped. Bent over, her hand on her knee for support. She couldn't do it. She couldn't go any further.

Something inside her—her father's expectations, her perceived failures, her banishment to St. Louis—mocked her. If she died tonight, Major Andrew McKenna would be proven right. She'd never amount to anything. She left no legacy other than a few award-winning photographs. She couldn't let that happen. She couldn't let him be right.

As she ran, she fumbled in her fanny pack.

Where is it? Where is it?

Her fingers brushed against her key ring and wrapped around it. With a last burst of energy fueled by fear and anger—and hope—she stumbled onto the stairs. The leather soles of her cowboy boots slipped on the wrought-iron steps and she fell to her knees. Got up. Fell again.

No traction!

Grabbing hold of the railing, hand over hand she pulled herself upward. At last, she staggered onto the top landing.

When she'd left for the powwow, it was daylight. She'd forgotten to turn on the porch light. Shadows filled the entryway. She fumbled with a key, but it wouldn't go into the lock.

Did she have the right one? She felt along the key ring, fingering each key.

There!

Someone bounded up the steps behind her. She wanted to scream, but her lungs burned from lack of oxygen. She quickly glanced behind her. Something moved fast in the darkness.

She pushed the newly-found key at the lock. It jammed.

Slow down. Slow down.

She tried again. He was almost upon her.

Hurry. Hurry.

The key slid in.

With a twist of the knob, she dove inside and slammed the door. The lock engaged automatically. Pressing her back against the cool wooden panel, she slid down until she sat with a plop on the floor. Her trembling legs sprawled out on the foyer rug. She didn't think she'd ever get up again.

What now?

First breathe. Then call the police.

Her dead cell phone lay on the nightstand next to her bed. Her house phone sat inside her living room doorway, out of reach.

Besides, what would she say when she got through to them? "Gee, Officer, an Indian by the name of Four Bears tried to kill me."

What did he look like, ma'am?

"He wore feathers and moccasins and war paint."

So did several hundred other Indians at the powwow.

She sat there a moment, thinking, fighting the urge to cry. Sweat poured down her face and burned the scratches inflicted by the saplings she'd plowed through. Her head ached. Her lungs burned from lack of oxygen. But it all attested to the fact she was alive. For the moment.

Holding her breath a second, she listened. Everything was quiet on the porch. When he saw he could no longer get to her, did he leave? Or was he waiting silently in the darkness? Waiting for her to open the door.

She set the camera on the floor next to the wall. If he did try to crash his way in, it was best not to be encumbered. Releasing the clasp on the fanny pack, she laid it next to the camera.

A pounding on the door reverberated from one end of the apartment to the other and sent shock waves through her.

He was knocking to be let in. To kill her. How polite.

"Shea, let me in."

Blade!

"Shea, please."

Standing up, she pressed her ear against the door. All her questions about his guilt thrust into her as if the knife blade had reached its mark. Had he seen Four Bears? Were they in this together? Was Blade trying to trick her—to gain access to kill her?

"Please," he said in a gentler voice. "We need to talk."

She groaned. She wanted to trust him, but he turned hot then cold for no apparent reason. Where was he when she needed him?

When the knife just missed her? When Four Bears chased her through the forest?

But just because his friend was a killer, didn't mean Blade was.

She reached for the doorknob, then hesitated. What should she do? Who could she trust? She started to hyperventilate.

Quiet settled again outside the door.

Had he gone? The thought of him turning away, hurt by her mistrust, pained her far more than she expected. With a shaky hand she turned on the porch light, engaged the chain lock, and inched open the door.

"Thanks," he said.

She searched his face for a hint of treachery. What did deceit look like on a face that handsome? His expression radiated concern. She supposed every murderer on death row looked just as determined and sincere when they lured their victims into trusting them.

His jaw tightened. "Please. Let me in."

She watched his mouth move as he spoke, remembering those lips kissing her, teasing her, saying gentle things to her. And those dark expressive eyes, filled now with worry.

Those eyes. She trusted those eyes.

"Are you alone?" she asked, tilting her head sideways to peek behind him.

Alarm flared in his eyes. "You're hurt!"

The porch light had revealed the burning welts and scratches on her face. Touching her forehead, she winced. Her hand came away wet with blood. Conscious of how she must look, she took inventory of her body. Nothing seemed to be broken, but she was covered head to toe with scratches, twigs, and leaves.

"I fell. In the woods. On the steps."

"Let me in. I have to see you're okay."

She leaned her head against the door. "I don't know who to trust."

He slipped his fingers through the opening and touched her cheek. "You can trust me, Shea. Let me help you."

Tears welled in her eyes, but she didn't move.

He slumped against the doorjamb. "I'll explain everything—from the beginning—while we fix you up. Please, just don't make me stand out here worrying about you."

All the fight had gone out of her. His words, his touch, were so soothing. She believed him. Unfortunately, she'd believed that bullfighter in Madrid. And the violinist who played for the Philharmonic. And the—well, she couldn't always trust her judgment when it came to matters of the heart. This time it could cost her life.

She gazed into his eyes. "Step back."

Closing the door, she disengaged the chain lock. Then opening it wide, she flicked on the foyer light and backed away.

Thirty-Four

Blade stepped into the foyer, took one look at her, and scooped her up in his arms. "Where's your bathroom?"

She motioned down the hall and laid her head against his shoulder. He carried her to the basin and put her down.

Turning on the light, she looked in the mirror. "Oh, my god."

Blood ran down the side of her face where the rock struck. Twigs and leafs stuck out of her hair at odd angles. Although she had tried to shield her face, red welts from striking branches crisscrossed her arms and neck. Tears and sweat had caused her mascara to run in a crazy zigzag pattern down her cheeks. She looked like the evil Indian spirit Manitou.

Blade ran hot water into the sink, opened the medicine cabinet, and took out cotton balls, sterilized pads, tape, medicated ointment, and Band-Aids. He grabbed a washcloth and towel from a rack. Lathering the cloth with soap, he turned back to her.

"This is going to hurt me more than you," he said.

"I don't think so."

He smiled and kissed her tenderly on the lips. Then he carefully dabbed at the wound on her forehead. "Maybe we should go to the hospital and get you stitches."

"I'm not going to a hospital. Just tape me up, coach, and get me in fighting shape."

His kiss had done wonders. She felt better already. Still, she kept an eye on him for any sudden moves. She hadn't a clue what she'd do if that happened.

He kissed her again. "Brave girl."

"There was no hospital in the jungles of Borneo when I fell from a tree and sprained my ankle. I still got the photograph of the orangutan. The local witch doctor taped my foot and I was good to go." She couldn't let him think she was a wuss. "And there was no hospital in the Himalayas when my Sherpa guide feared I had frost bite. He soaked my hands in lukewarm water and I survived. There was—"

Blade kissed her again and continued to dress her wounds. "I don't want to hear about Borneo or orangutans or the Himalayas. I want to know what happened tonight."

Shea told him everything. As she talked, he cleaned, medicated, and bandaged abrasions. Then kissed her cheek, her neck, her wrist, wherever a wound. Bandaged another injury and kissed her again. She found it difficult to think clearly.

He interrupted her only once when he said, "I'm going to have to take your shirt off. To get at the blood that ran beneath your collar."

"Oh—okay."

His hands brushed against her breasts as he slowly unsnapped each pearl button. Her breath faltered. A long lock of his shiny hair fell forward and tickled her shoulder. She'd cooled down from her run through the forest, and now her body was heating up again—this time pleasantly.

He continued to work his magic as she talked. When she'd finished her tale, he held her close and kissed her on the mouth, then repeated her last words. "A Dog Soldier tried to kill you?"

She hesitated, knowing what she said next would stop the kisses. "Four Bears."

The concern in Blade's eyes changed to disbelief. "That can't be."

"He was dressed as a Dog Soldier."

"Him and fifty others." He stepped away from her.

"I saw him. Half of his face was painted black and half white." She thought a minute. "I questioned him earlier about you and the lance. He must have felt threatened."

Blade shook his head. "All I saw was you darting into the woods and a Dog Soldier go after you. I was too far away to recognize him, but I'm sure it wasn't Bear."

"I have him on film. I used the flash to blind him while I got away."

Blade threw the washcloth in the sink. "I guess now would be a good time to explain everything like I promised. But there's something I want to do first."

"What's that?"

He left the bathroom and headed for the front door. She followed. "Got a flashlight? I'm going back for the knife," he said.

"It probably won't be there. He swung one at me after I blinded him with the flash."

"You said you couldn't pull the knife from the tree. Maybe he couldn't either. Maybe he had a second knife."

Shea nodded, remembering that more than one Indian brave wore a knife at his waist and another tucked in his knee-high moccasins.

He opened the door, then kissed her on the forehead. "You stood by that big oak, right? I don't know if the knife's still there, but if it is, there'll be prints on the handle."

She didn't like the idea of him going back. "I tried to pull the knife from the tree. The prints might be smeared."

"I'm going for it."

Blade seemed determined. She fetched him a flashlight. The drums had stopped vibrating long ago. The tribes were tucked away in their tepees. She peeked out a narrow side light by the door. All was quite. And dark.

"Be careful."

"Will you be all right alone? I can still take you to the hospital."

"I'm fine."

This time his kiss was fiery. A tingling started in her toes and worked its way up. Letting go of her, he stepped outside. "I'll be right back."

Locking the door, she retrieved the camera and fanny pack from the floor and slipped into her bedroom. She deposited them on the bed, turned on the lamp on her nightstand, and picked up the phone extension sitting next to the clock-radio.

She dialed Kathryn's private number. Her aunt answered on the second ring. "Hi, this is Kathryn."

"Listen, things have gotten—"

"I'm not able to come to the phone right now. At the tone, leave a message and I'll get back to you."

Rats! She must still be at the charity function.

She wants a message? I'll give her a message. Someone tried to kill me. They chased me through the woods. They tried to slice off my face. I'm bleeding.

"Call me," was all she said.

Returning the phone to its cradle, she pulled open the nightstand's bottom drawer. Inside, nestled between a mystery novel and a bottle of sleeping pills in case the novel didn't work, was a loaded .38 Smith & Wesson.

Thirty-Five

With all the bandages Blade had applied to her wounds, Shea was unable to take a much-needed shower. She stripped the rest of the way and washed the best she could. Donning a clean T-shirt and jeans, she tucked the gun in her waistband at the small of her back. Its weight and nearness reassured her in case she'd been wrong about Blade. Her aunt didn't raise a fool.

A raucous knocking on Shea's door announced his return.

She peeked through the side light to make sure. "Who is it," she said in a mischievous voice.

He shot her an exasperated look. "Let me in."

"Come in," she said, opening the door. "The neighbors might not understand a man dressed in loincloth and fringed breeches on my doorstep."

He moved inside. "At least you haven't lost your sense of humor."

"Gallows humor."

The foyer light shone across his muscular chest, exposing a rippling six-pack that sent a delightful buzz all through her bandaged body. She'd been too frightened before to notice. "Want to know the truth? I'm scared to death."

He smiled reassuringly. "You don't have to be afraid any more."

"Where's the knife?"

"I checked every tree at the edge of the forest. There was no knife. Just a gash in the tree you stood next to."

Her mouth turned dry as scorched earth. "There was a knife."

He reached for her. "I believe you."

She waved him away. "I'm fine. If Four Bears—or whoever—didn't retrieve the knife before going into the forest, they must've returned for it. Like you said, there would be prints."

"I believe you."

Sympathetic to the turmoil he must be experiencing, she softened her tone. "I want the truth about what's going on. Don't leave anything out."

He started to close the door.

"No. Leave it open."

She hated doubting him, but maybe *he* got rid of the knife because *his* prints were on it. She folded her arms across her chest, closing him off until she heard his story.

He gazed sadly at her and put his hands on his hips as if to keep from taking her into his arms. Despite everything, she ached to feel them around her.

He began his story. "Cheek Larson came to my studio in Santa Fe and made a proposal. The Missouri Westward Museum needed a recently purchased group of Indian artifacts restored. Besides our pay, they would donate money for a clinic on our reservation. I jumped at the offer.

"At the museum workshop, Larson instructed me to make replicas of certain artifacts. He explained they needed duplicates to conduct hands-on lectures for school children." Blade shook his head. "Like a fool I believed him."

"It's a legitimate request," she said, knowing this was a common practice. "Why didn't you remind Cullen right away about the duplicates?"

"Because after replicating two or three relics, I asked Cheek how Cullen liked them. Except for the lance I restored, Bear had done most of the work. I wanted him to get credit for his artistry. Cheek acted nervous and told me to keep my mouth shut. He'd put the fakes on the gallery wall and sold the relics to collectors here and in Europe. I threatened to go to the authorities.

Cheek said he'd tell them I was the one stealing the artifacts, and that he caught me. He'd worked with Cullen before, and Cullen trusted him."

Blade glanced away for a moment, then added, "I have a record. That's why my father wants me to talk to Wild Horse. As a teenager, I got in trouble with the law over some drunk and rowdy white men. They'd come onto the reservation for kicks, hurrahing our town and accosting our women."

"What'd you do?"

"Bear and I asked them to leave. Nicely. One of the men laughed and grabbed Bear's sister. He won't be doing that again. But the white men told the white man's law we'd attacked them outside the reservation. That it was Bear and I who were drunk and causing trouble. What chance did I have with Jansen if he learned about my record?"

She nodded, relaxing her arms.

Blade continued, "I realized Bear would go to prison along with me, and I couldn't let that happen. I was willing to face up to my part in the scheme, even if I was an innocent participant, but Bear and the rest of the tribe shouldn't have to pay for my mistake. The museum would never donate the money for the clinic, not to mention the shame that would fall on the tribe because their future chief was accused of being a thief."

Shea appreciated his dilemma and why he felt he couldn't confide in her. Innocent people would've suffered if he misplaced his trust. He couldn't take that chance.

"Cheek." Blade breathed the name as if it were a foul epithet. "Now I know how a trapped animal feels. Until I found a way to clear our names, I had to protect my men and the artifacts. If the relics left American soil, they'd be lost to the Indian forever."

"Ann told me how valuable they are on the European market."

Blade nodded. "Bear and I made two replicas instead of one. One fake went to the museum, and one went to Cheek. The other registrar isn't as experienced as Ethan. The fakes slipped past her. I kept the real artifacts hidden in the locked sleeping room at the workshop until I could manage to replace the fakes on the museum walls and in showcases with the real thing. We planned to disassemble the duplicates and put the materials back into our supply inventory piece by piece." He smiled at her. "That's why I couldn't let you and Ann go into the sleeping room."

She understood now.

Blade's voice took on a note of pride. "Bear and I did our best work ever replicating the artifacts. The tribe's future depended on it. But I hadn't accounted for Ethan's expert eye."

Shea held her breath. Was Blade about to tell her he killed Ethan to shut him up? She wanted to warn him not to say another word, to go now, go back to the reservation, hide. But she knew he wouldn't. Even if he'd murdered Ethan in a moment of weakness, or for the good of the tribe, she knew he'd stay and face the consequences. Otherwise, why tell her all this?

"Go on," she said, dreading he would.

"When Ethan went to Ann and Cullen with the lance," Blade said, "I knew there'd be an investigation. I had to hide the real relics somewhere besides the workshop. I remembered an old Indian saying. 'Where is the best place to hide a leaf?' The answer is 'on a tree.' That night, Bear and I took the hidden artifacts to the museum, but not to the storeroom as we told the guard. Even though the timing was dangerous, we took them to the new gallery and replaced the fakes with the real thing as we'd planned to do all along. We then took the fakes to the student classroom. That's why Bennett found genuine artifacts on the gallery walls."

"Smart."

Was that the same cunning he used to kill Ethan? He'd just admitted he and Four Bears were in the museum the night the old man died. She knew he was telling the truth, because at the powwow, Four Bears confessed to helping his chief that fatal night. Had he helped to replace the fake relics or kill Ethan or both?

"I also replaced the three reproductions with other relics.

Cheek had already stolen the originals. So many items are on display, without checking the catalog sheets, no one would know the difference."

Her thoughts jumped back to the night Ethan died. On her way to Ann's office, she'd seen two dark figures at the gallery entrance. Joe, the custodian, had seen two Indians in the gallery, also. Was it Blade and Four Bears? If they'd seen her, would they have killed her, too? Was that why Ethan was murdered? He'd interrupted their plan and accused them of stealing artifacts?

This had gone on long enough. She had to know. Now.

"Who killed Ethan?"

Thirty-Six

"I don't know who killed Ethan," Blade said.

Shea's heart did a flip. "You said you were responsible."

"I am. If I'd gone to the police right away, before Ethan discovered the fake lance, he'd still be alive. I blame myself for his death."

She sighed with relief. Everything was right with the world. But *someone* killed Ethan.

"I understand why you think that." She touched his arm to encourage him. "But if anyone's to blame, it's Four Bears or Cheek. Cheek contrived the whole thing, forcing Four Bears to silence Ethan while he was in Santa Fe. Then Four Bears tried to kill me to protect you."

Blade shook his head, unwilling to believe this of his friend. She saw the skepticism in his eyes. He'd asked her to trust him. Would he trust her, or would he stick by Four Bears? She appreciated the reassuring feel of the gun in her waistband.

"Where are Cheek and Four Bears now?" she said.

"I don't know. Most of the time, I was in the sweat lodge meditating. Praying to the Great Spirit and my ancestors for any ideas on getting me out of this mess."

"Did they have an answer?"

Although she didn't believe in such things, she didn't want to dash his hopes. In fact, she said a quick, silent prayer of her own. If it worked, she'd have to rethink her faltering faith in something higher than her own self-reliance. Right now, she wasn't doing too well.

"I had a vision." He reached for her.

She let him take her into his arms. His warm skin electrified her. She forgot she'd ever doubted him. He'd vowed he hadn't murdered Ethan, and she believed him. She had to trust somebody.

"In the vision," he said, "my ancestors said a beautiful woman with hair the color of burnished copper would help me." He entwined a lock of her dark auburn hair around his finger.

She smiled. "Is that right?"

He pulled her tight against him. She felt his body respond to hers.

"My ancestors said this woman would give me comfort."

His lips brushed against her cheek. Her legs felt shaky, and she leaned into him.

"My ancestors said—"

"Look," she breathed. Her words took on a throaty quality. "The foyer's getting awfully crowded with you, me, and your ancestors. Why don't we just speak our minds?"

"That's what I'm doing." He kissed her neck.

He was doing a lot more than that.

"Okay, why'd you treat me so coldly at the workshop and in the museum storeroom with Cheek?"

She tried to sound mad from the remembered slight, but his lips were inching toward hers. Nibbling her neck, her cheek, kissing the corner of her mouth.

"I feared for your safety," he managed somewhere between nibbles and kisses. "After what happened to Ethan and Cullen, Cheek said if I got too friendly with you, told you anything, you'd be next."

He kissed her eyelids. She found it difficult to think.

Concentrate.

After Ethan revealed the fake lance, Cheek demanded that Blade meet him outside.

Right.

Cheek was at the police interrogation, Tom Bennett's verification of the artifacts, the search of Blade's workshop, and in the museum storeroom.

Yes.
Moonlit nights, red wine, and the scent of roses.
No, no.
He was nibbling her ear.
Get back on track. Concentrate.
Each time Cheek was with them, Blade acted cool toward her. When Cheek was absent—at the tepee in the gallery, at the Patrons Ball, at the zoo, and now—Blade lavished attention on her.

Inside the tepee in the gallery, when he first took you into his arms—boy, he can kiss.

She pulled back from hormonal-induced oblivion. "Cheek couldn't have done all this alone," she said, pushing Blade away.

Except for a few ruffled feathers, he looked completely in control. On the other hand, she once again was finding it difficult to breath.

Get control.

"Ethan's dead," she said. "Cullen's wounded. And Four Bears—someone—tried to kill *me* tonight. Ann and Cheek don't get along well enough to be partners in crime. And you claim you were duped into making the fakes. That leaves Billy, Elk Horn, and—as much as you hate to admit it—Four Bears."

He pulled her to him again. This pushing away and pulling together was making her dizzy. Or was it having his arms around her that caused her light-headedness?

"I've known Bear all my life," he whispered against the soft flesh of her throat. He ran his hands down her back to her hips, pressing her closer. "I can't believe he'd kill Ethan."

"Not even if he feels it's for a just cause?" She ran her fingers through his long hair and draped it over her shoulders. "He believes the relics should be returned to the Indians."

"Let's talk about something else," he whispered.

He ran his hands across her hips. She returned the favor, grabbing hold of his bare buttocks. He maneuvered her down the hall toward her bedroom. "Or let's not talk at all," he said.

"No. No, we have to get this straightened out before someone else gets hurt."

He sighed and leaned his forehead against hers. "Bear hates Cheek. He hates that he passes himself off as an Indian."

"Part Indian," she corrected.

He raised back. "Not even part. It's all an act. He thinks the museum and Indians will trust him more. That he'll get better deals if we believe he's one of us."

He ran his hands under her T-shirt and around to the small of her back, pulling her tight against him again.

Wrapping a leg around his, she fought for air.

Keep talking. Think. Think. Otherwise, they were about to get to the point of no return. This time she doubted she could stop him—or herself.

"Do Ann and Cullen know?" she asked.

"I don't know. I thought it was a harmless business practice." He nuzzled her ear. "I didn't know then he dealt in the black market. Now I wonder if he's been cheating Cullen and my people all along."

"Cullen trusts Cheek. Ann trusts Cullen. I trust Ann. No one wants to believe someone they trust has lied to them."

"Do you trust me?" he asked.

She tightened her hold on him and pulled his face close to hers. She ran her tongue across his parted lips, then kissed him eagerly.

"I'll take that as a yes," he said when they came up for air.

"Oh, yes."

His arms encircled her waist and he picked her up, holding her tightly against him. She wrapped both her legs around his hips. She could feel his lean, hard body meld with hers. Tiny kachina dolls with prickly feet ran down her spine.

"Is that a gun in your waistband?" he asked between kisses.

"Uh-huh."

His warm, hungry mouth found hers.

She reached out with a foot and kicked the door shut. She was no longer in danger.

Then again, maybe she was in more danger than she'd ever been.

Thirty-Seven

Shea pressed her body against Blade's with an urgency that rivaled his. His lips hungrily searched her throat, her cheeks, her eyelids, then devoured her mouth with an intensity that left her weak and wanting more. She felt herself slipping dangerously past that point of no return.

A glimmer of accountability forced itself into the mix. How could she be thinking of making hot monkey love to Blade while Ethan's killer was still on the loose? She was no closer to finding the responsible party than when she'd stopped him from taking her into the bedroom.

"We can't do this," she said with every ounce of moral strength she could muster. Reluctantly, she let her legs slide down his thighs till her feet hit the foyer floor.

"I know." He kissed her one last time.

She believed with all her heart that Blade was *not* the killer. Then who was?

His response registered.

"Wait a minute. You agree?"

He didn't have to cave in to her demand for restraint so quickly. Especially since she wasn't sure she'd made the right decision. Granted, it'd been a long time since she'd been in a serious relationship, but surely her sexual radar hadn't atrophied that badly.

"I promised my ancestors," he said, turning her loose.

"That's a new one. Your ancestors? Not your tribe or father or church?"

Embarrassed at being rejected, she adjusted her clothes and smoothed her hair. What was she crabbing about? He'd been gentlemanly enough to respect her wishes. No means no, right?

Still, he could've acted a little disappointed.

"I promised my ancestors I would concentrate solely on finding Ethan's murderer if they would guide me. Before anyone else is hurt." He looked into her eyes. "That's what *you* said, too. Have you changed your mind?"

"Of course not. That's what I said. Except for the ancestors."

He kissed her nose. "I promised not to let anything—or anyone—distract me."

She snuggled closer. "Am I distracting?"

Blade moaned. "Very. Believe me. That was the hardest promise I've ever had to keep. As soon as I fulfill my obligation to clear my name and return respectability to my tribe, I intend to pick up where we left off. If that's all right with you," he added, amusement flickering in his eyes.

She felt her smile brighten a few kilowatts. "Then let's get busy."

Clothes adjusted and feathers secured, they retired to the living room couch.

"So, what do we do first?" she asked. "Er, now."

"Take a cold shower?"

She laughed. "Want a Pepsi? Or how about tea? I'll put on a kettle of water to heat and be right back."

When she returned, they settled on the couch in the living room.

"I've told you what I know," he said. "Maybe if we pool our information, something will stand out."

"Okay, let's look at what we know for sure. Cheek admitted to selling the artifacts on the European black market. And Four Bears tried to kill me tonight."

"*Someone* dressed like a Dog Soldier tried to kill you," he corrected.

She thought if he heard her say that enough times, he'd believe her. "All right, *someone* tried to kill me."

She had to admit, there'd been a lot of Dog Soldiers at the powwow.

"And someone tried to kill Cullen," Blade said.

She nodded. "Ann confided that she and Cullen were together all night after he'd returned from Santa Fe. They have a thing. Evidently his ancestors aren't as involved as yours," she explained in response to Blade's confused look. "That leaves Cheek without an alibi for the time Ethan was murdered and exposes him as a liar." She smiled reassuringly at Blade. "That should help prove your word against his."

"I don't think Lieutenant Jansen will see it that way."

"Okay, you and Four Bears were together. You alibi each other."

"Or Jansen will think we're both guilty."

She pursed her lips. "I was wandering around the museum trying to find Ethan and Ann. The guard saw me leave through the front door. Alone. Ignoring Jansen's suspicions that Ann and I are another Thelma and Louise, I had no reason to kill Ethan. And Ann was with Cullen. So that leaves Cheek and whoever is in this with him."

"Whoever? You mean Bear, don't you?"

"Would you rather it's Billy or Elk Horn? Besides, neither of them dressed as a Dog Soldier. I saw the person chasing me in the glare of the camera flash."

Blade shook his head. "I still can't believe Bear would do this. He's as adamant as I am that Indian relics should be returned to the Indian Nation. He wouldn't help Cheek steal them to be sold on the European market."

"I didn't want to believe Ann was guilty either. Then Jansen accused her. And there were times when she looked at Cullen with such puppy-dog eyes I thought maybe, just maybe, she could be a hapless dupe. She might not have realized what was going on until someone murdered Ethan. Then it was too late to turn back." She paused, then asked, "What is a Dog Soldier?"

"They were the elite warriors of the tribe. The last line of defense. They wore a sash that trailed the ground and impaled it with a sacred arrow during battle. Pinned to that spot, the Dog Soldier sang a song they alone could sing as they fought to their death."

"Wow. That's certainly impressive."

"Only a coward would dress as a Dog Soldier and kill a woman. Or an old man such as Ethan."

"I agree."

"That's not Bear. So what are we going to tell Jansen?"

She took a deep breath and held up a finger. "First, that Cheek had a motive to kill Ethan. He wanted to cover up the fact he stole the relics and sold them.

"Second," she waggled two fingers, "Cheek had the opportunity. He and Cullen returned from Santa Fe during the night, earlier than expected. They went to the museum. Cullen left with Ann. Cheek happened upon Ethan with the lance in a dark hallway."

She fluttered three fingers in front of Blade. He made a swipe to catch them, but she eluded his grasp. "Which brings us to number three. Means. Ethan was carrying the lance when he ran into Cheek. A handy weapon, Cheek used it to kill him. There's no doubt in my mind that Cheek is strong enough to drive a lance through a man as thin and frail as Ethan."

"And cowardly enough," Blade added.

She nodded. "Maybe Ethan confronted Cheek again about the forgery, and Cheek killed him. But he was frightened away before he retrieved the lance from Ethan's body. Maybe when I walked to my car."

Blade finally caught hold of her fingers and kissed them. "Motive, means, and opportunity." He kissed the palm of her hand. Then her wrist, working his way up her arm.

"Stop it," she said with little conviction. "I can't think when you do that. Besides, your ancestors are watching." She kissed him and pushed him away. "We have to concentrate on getting you out of this mess."

"I know, I know," he agreed. "Okay, what you said about Cheek sounds plausible, but will Jansen buy it? Cheek can turn the whole thing around and claim Bear or I killed Ethan for the same reason. And because Cullen worked with Cheek before, the director trusts him."

"Well, then we'll just have to convince Cullen before we go to Jansen."

"How?"

She thought a moment, then snapped her fingers. "Ann. If I can convince her, she'll help me convince Cullen."

She snatched up a pen and pad of paper from a table next to the couch. "Write down the three relics that Cheek stole before you realized what he was doing. I'll show Ann those particular items aren't displayed on the gallery walls and they're not in the storeroom. She can check the catalog sheets and the photos I took. Where did you say the reproductions are?"

"Two of the items, a beaded medicine pouch and a rawhide tom-tom, we disassembled and put the pieces back into scrap inventory. Only the duplicate of the ceremonial pipe went to the children's learning room after Ethan discovered the fake lance. Later we added the authentic lance, which Jansen now has along with the fake, and the replica of the buffalo hide shield."

"All right. Ann will see the duplicates. But how do we convince her some originals are gone?"

"As soon as we put the word out that Cheek sold fake relics as the genuine article," he said, "there'll be an uproar from the buyers."

"That's right. His customers may not know the items were stolen. They probably thought their dealings with Cheek were legitimate. They'll jump at the chance to get even with him and get their money back. We'll match what they return with the catalog sheets and photos to show her they were originally in the museum's inventory."

"I'll go with you to talk to Ann," he offered. "If she sees I'm willing to come forward with this, she'll be more apt to believe you."

"That's true, but we also need to keep an eye on Cheek. He's already killed one person. Who knows what he'll do next? He's too dangerous to be allowed to run loose."

Blade pulled her to her feet. "Call Ann and arrange a meeting. My men and I will find Cheek. I'll have them keep him at the workshop until you and I talk to Ann. I'll meet you back here once we have Cheek corralled."

"Be careful," she warned him once again. She couldn't stand it if something happened to him. "Cheek killed once. He won't hesitate to kill again."

He cupped her face in his hands and kissed her. "Don't worry. Remember, in the sweat lodge my ancestors said a woman with red hair would help me clear my name." He smiled at her. "They've been right so far."

She clung to him. "Remember, Cheek wasn't in this alone."

He kissed her again. "Wait for me."

Thirty-Eight

After Blade left, Shea phoned Ann to set up their meeting. Cullen answered on the first ring.

"Oh. Cullen. Is Ann, uh, busy?"

"I'm sorry, Shea," he said, "but Ann's in the shower. Can I help?"

With no time to waste, she related everything Blade told her about the forgeries. She hoped Cullen would keep an open mind.

"Your accusations are outrageous," he said. "Cheek and I have worked together at other museums. We've never had any problems. Why would he want to ruin his reputation and mine?"

"It does sound bad, but it's the only explanation I can come up with. Don't wait until Monday to check the catalog sheets and photos. We can verify immediately that three relics are missing. Then issue a statement to the press. I guarantee it won't be long before we hear from whomever Cheek sold the artifacts to. Fake or real."

"And if you're wrong, you've slandered one of the best dealers I've ever worked with. The museum would lose a valuable source of relics."

"But who else could have murdered Ethan?" she asked, knowing full well who he'd suggest.

He didn't fail her. "Blade Santee. He could have concocted this story to cover his tracks. I've never dealt with the Dakota chieftain before, so I can't vouch for him. You know how militant these Indians get about their relics. What a wonderful opportunity for them to raise money for a medical clinic and retrieve the artifacts at the same time. I can imagine how they're laughing behind our backs."

She wished there was some way she could convince him of Blade's innocence. She had nothing more to go on than his word, but she couldn't tell Cullen. It would only cause him to doubt her judgment. As he suggested, Blade and Four Bears could've pulled off everything. Lieutenant Jansen would determine it more plausible that Four Bears and Blade were partners in crime than Four Bears and Cheek.

Her thoughts spun. What could she say to convince Cullen to check the catalog for missing relics? At least they'd be back on track that Ethan's murder wasn't some random mugging.

"Cullen, someone tried to kill you."

"Yes, that's a troubling point. And I'm sure Jansen is being coy by not mentioning it. He gives us enough rope to hang ourselves."

She agreed. She'd seen the wily detective use the same ploy during his interrogation in the museum conference room. They'd been at each other's throats like vultures on a day-old carcass.

"Besides," he said, "you heard what I think. As soon as the Indians return to their reservation, I'll no longer be in danger."

"I hope you're right. But what if you're not?"

"Look, I don't want to seem unfair," he said. "Where are you?"

"At my apartment across from the park."

"Are you alone?"

"Yes."

"Okay, why don't we do this? Meet me at the back of the museum. We'll check the catalog and photos. I don't want to involve Ann until I know more. She's finally calmed down after all that's happened. I don't want to upset her again unnecessarily."

Shea found Cullen's concern for Ann touching. Her opinion of him softened.

"Thank you, Cullen. I owe you one."

"Don't be too quick to thank me. If relics *are* missing, I'm going straight to the police, no matter who's guilty. I have my own reputation to protect. It could be we'll find Blade or one of his tribesmen sold the relics. Do you know where he is now?"

"He went to find his men." She wasn't about to tell Cullen that Blade planned on corralling Cheek. She didn't want kidnapping added to the list of charges against him.

"Good. Come alone. Until I know who's responsible, I'm less likely to get another knife stuck in me if we keep this between us."

If Shea could get Cullen on her side before she talked to Ann, all the better. She'd leave a note on the door letting Blade know she'd gone to the museum to check the catalog sheets. He could meet her there.

Thirty-Nine

Shea parked next to Cullen's empty silver Bentley. No other cars remained in the museum lot. Well after midnight, the guards and cleaning crew had left.

"No doubt tucked safely in their beds," she muttered. Right where she should be.

She scanned the unlighted pathway leading to the building's back door. Sitting alone behind a dark, deserted museum after someone tried to kill her ranked right up there with photographing bloated animal carcasses along a flooded Senegalese River.

In the distance, once again the tom-toms thrummed. The eerie trill of an Indian flute drifted on the night air. The powwow was over. Something had disturbed the camp.

Warily, she got out of the car. Flinching at every snapping twig and rustling bush, she made her way across the shadowy lawn.

The museum's back door stood ajar.

"Cullen," she called.

No answer.

She glanced around to see if anyone was watching and pushed the door the rest of the way open. "Cullen?"

Getting no response, she stepped inside.

The alarm system had been turned off, its panel of colored lights extinguished. If Cullen were here, why didn't he answer? He'd said to meet him by the back door.

Maybe he couldn't answer.

The hairs on the back of her neck stood up. She pulled the .38 Smith & Wesson from her waistband.

"Cullen, if you're okay, I need you to answer me. Now."

Nothing.

He could've gone to the new gallery to start checking the relics. Or to Ann's office for the catalog sheets. Or maybe he was hurt and needed help.

Skimming a hand along the marble wall for guidance, Shea made her way down the dimly lit hallways. If he were okay, why hadn't he turned on the lights?

Because he didn't want anyone to know what he and Shea were doing until they found the proof they were looking for. That's what he'd told her over the phone. She relaxed and continued on to the Indian gallery.

Streetlights outside the room's French windows cast eerie shadows on the marble floor. In the distance, tribal drums pulsated. She peered through one of the floor-to-ceiling panes at the stone terrace and fountain where Blade and she danced Friday night. She could almost hear the strains of a Viennese waltz and smell his natural cologne of leather and smoke. The memory of his arms around her sent her pulse racing. She had to help him clear his name.

Scanning the displays for a sign of Cullen, Shea walked deeper into the cavernous room. She worked her way past the stuffed buffalo, dugout canoe, and tepee. A statue of an Indian with raised tomahawk looked almost real in the moonlit shadows. Displayed near a window, the white leather coat once worn by Manuel Lisa appeared iridescent in the streetlight's glimmer, almost as if the ghost of the Spanish fur trader still wore it. Despite the room's hot, stuffy atmosphere, the glint of finely-honed weapons hanging on the walls sent a shiver through her.

Out of the corner of her eye, she saw something silvery stir in the dark by the gallery entrance. She spun toward it.

"Cullen, is that you? Cullen?"

Getting no answer, she remained quiet. Why would he hide? Unless it wasn't Cullen.

A cold sweat trickled down her back. Her breathing became labored. Her hands waxed clammy. The gun slipped. She clutched it tighter. Raising it, she aimed toward the gallery entrance. Anyone could have found the museum door open and come in, including whoever killed Ethan. Shea looked at the gun. Could she kill someone if her life was in danger?

A spasm of fear shot through her. Her own principles might get her killed. It was stupid to come here alone. She'd sneak back out and wait for Blade.

Stepping behind the stuffed buffalo, she bent low and circled alongside the canoe. The route would take her to the hallway. Maybe, in the dark, she could dart past whoever was there and make a run for safety.

A noise by the gallery entrance stopped her. The white shadowy form she'd glimpsed took on the vague shape of a man advancing toward her. She remembered how she'd scared herself a few nights ago with her own reflection in a glass showcase. She glanced at Manuel Lisa's white knee-length coat, but the mannequin stood at wrong angles to cast a reflection near the entrance. Besides, there were no glass showcases there, just weapons on the wall, weapons the intruder could use to kill her.

She took a deep breath and steadied the gun. Cautiously, she maneuvered behind the Indian statue.

"Shea, darling," Cullen's voice called. The silvery shape solidified into the director in his dove-gray suit. "Quit flitting about."

She heaved a sigh of relief and stepped from behind the statue. "Cullen! You scared the life out of me."

"I'm sorry. I'd gone to Ann's office to get the catalog sheets, but she must have locked them in the vault. I suppose we'll have to retrieve them in the morning."

In an effort to soothe her frazzled nerves, Shea leaned against the statue. Instead of cold, unyielding marble, warm, viable flesh breathed beneath the period clothing. She jerked away as if she'd touched a live rattlesnake and gaped up at the Indian on the pedestal.

He wore a feathered coyote headdress that hung across his broad back. The lower half of his scowling face was painted white; the upper half, black. A Bowie knife hung from his waist. She choked back a scream as the Dog Soldier stepped down from his perch.

Forty

"Oh, dear," Cullen said in a voice turned cold and mocking. "You've found Cheek. I guess we'll just have to kill you now."

Shea twisted toward Cullen, then back to Cheek. Her mind raced to reshuffle the suspects in Ethan's murder. Cullen and Cheek. Not Blade. Not Ann. Not Four Bears or any of the other Indians. It was Cullen and Cheek.

"I won't actually do the killing," Cullen corrected himself. "I let Cheek take care of the messy stuff. Wouldn't want to soil my clothes." He brushed at an imaginary smudge on his suit. "Besides, he enjoys it so much."

An apparition from a bad dream, Cheek moved with power and determination. Shea backed away, but the evasive move put her directly between the hulking dealer and Cullen. A squeeze play. She fought back the panic rioting inside her.

"You and Cheek? Together?" she questioned, stalling until she thought of a feasible escape. She could shoot one of them, but the other would be upon her before she could dispatch him.

"Oh, of course," Cullen sneered. "And not only this one, but quite a few scams at other museums before I came here. And without a hitch, I might add. Cheek and I have been doing business for some time. If that silly twit Ann hadn't hired you and Brumley, we would've gotten away with our little ruse once again."

"And Blade?"

She had to know the truth. In her heart, Shea believed in his innocence, but she wanted to hear it from someone who had nothing to gain by lying. Even though she may not live to see the handsome Indian again.

Cullen let out a low, malevolent chuckle. "Who'd have thought Blade would've turned out to be such an honest Injun?"

Shea sighed with relief. She could die happy. Well, not exactly. "But someone tried to kill you."

"A ploy to divert attention away from my own guilt. Cheek's equally good with knife or tomahawk. Why don't you show her, Cheek?"

Her gun was pointed at Cullen. She swung the barrel toward Cheek, but not before he flung the tomahawk at her. It knocked the gun from her hand and sent it skidding under a glass showcase. Grinning, he pulled the knife from his waistband and advanced toward her.

"You'll never get away with this," she warned, sounding like a cliché from an old movie. Slowly, she backed toward the spot where her gun disappeared. "How will you explain my death?"

Cullen chuckled. "We'll wipe Cheek's prints from the knife and drop this red feather next to your lifeless body. Just like we did with the phony attempt on my life." He held up a feather similar to the one Blade wore. Clearly caught up in the humor of it all, he added. "That fool Ann even bought a gun. To protect me, no less."

A voice constricted with pain and anger cut short his laughter. "My money won't be wasted."

Ann walked determinedly down the corridor toward them, her handgun leveled on Cullen's back.

He spun around. "Ann!"

Cheek halted his advance on Shea and turned his attention to the curator.

Shea edged out of the line of fire. Someone was about to be hurt, and the odds were no longer in the men's favor. Two women plus one gun beat two men with a knife. Maybe. At least she hoped so. Her gun hadn't fared so well.

Cullen sneered. "What a comedy of errors. Don't place your

hopes of rescue on Ann, Shea. She was afraid to even load the gun. I did it for her." Moonlight streaming through the windows illuminated his evil grin. "And then I unloaded it while she was in the shower."

"You're bluffing," Ann said.

"Try me, love."

She pointed the gun at his crotch.

Shea thought she detected a slight flinching of Cullen's decorum.

Two hollow clicks echoed through the gallery. Stunned, Ann stared at the empty gun. Her hand went limp. The useless weapon fell with a clatter to the marble floor.

Shea dived at Cullen as he turned toward her. She buried her right shoulder in the pit of his stomach. Photographing Japanese sumo wrestlers for *Big Men* magazine had paid off in more ways than one.

Cullen crashed backward through one of the French windows. He landed with a bone-jarring thud on the stone terrace.

Shea spun and dove for her gun under the showcase. The tips of her fingers grazed the .38's wooden grip. She couldn't quite reach…

At the sound of heavy breathing close behind her, she rolled away and jumped to her feet. Without the gun.

Cheek lurched after her.

"Run, Ann," she shouted and feigned a rush at the dealer.

Fast on her feet from dodging bulls on the streets of Pamplona, Shea evaded his clumsy lunges. What was one awkward mouth-breather when he didn't have Cullen's brains to back him up? She soon found out that he was a mean, mad maniac.

He thrust the knife, swishing it in front of her face.

She leapt backward.

Ann screamed, frozen in place.

Shea backed deeper into the gallery, drawing Cheek away from her friend. She wouldn't be able to hold him off for long. "Run, Ann," she shouted again.

Ann stood rigidly still.

"Don't go brain dead on me now," Shea coaxed.

Cheek glanced over his shoulder at Ann.

"No, no. Here," Shea taunted and retreated farther into the room. "Come on. Come and get me."

Her last words escaped in a grunt as she backed into the stuffed buffalo.

In the unguarded moment, Cheek threw himself at her. The knife blade sliced the air inches from her throat. Dodging, she tripped over the bow of the hollowed-out canoe and fell inside. Her heart convulsed as she realized she'd never make it out of the dugout before he reached her.

His thick lips twisted into a cruel, wet grin. Standing erect, he spoke for the first time since she'd entered the gallery.

"*Akoana.*"

The Sioux word for goodbye.

Shea groped for something—anything—to hold him off. Her hand raked over the paddle lying in the bottom of the canoe. Half of it rested beneath her.

Cheek's grin slipped into a smirk.

Fear coursed through her. Wiggling around, she jerked on the paddle's handle. It wouldn't budget.

He leaned into the canoe. She smelled the stench of his sweat mixed with whiskey on his breath.

Oh, god help me. She rolled on her side and jerked the paddle free just as the blade of Cheek's Bowie knife arced toward her. It dug into the ancient wood and slammed the paddle against her cheek.

Growling like some wild animal, he pulled the knife backward over his head with the paddle still attached. The slab of wood broke loose from her grip and sailed into one of the glass showcases, shattering it into a thousand pieces.

With renewed rage, he again swung the knife at Shea. This time there was nothing left to protect her.

"No!" she shouted, as if that would stop him.

Her life flashed before her in Kodak moments, mostly filled with water buffalos and gun bearers and Chinese junkets and sumo wrestlers. Other than her family and one close friend who stood screaming on the other side of the room, no one special popped into mind who would weep at her funeral. No one else cared about what happened to her, except maybe…

Through Cheek's straddled legs, she saw Blade quietly enter the gallery. He clamped a hand over Ann's mouth and moved her out of harm's way. Hope must have shown on Shea's face, because Cheek halted and stared at her in confusion.

"Cheek," Blade shouted in a commanding voice that could raise the dead.

Hatred and fury contorted Cheek's features. Forgetting Shea, the dealer whirled to face the Dakota chieftain.

"Santee." He spat out the name like a curse. "You've been a problem too long. You tricked me with the fake artifacts. I'd have killed you long ago if Cullen hadn't been so greedy for more relics. Now you think you're going to cheat me out of my fun? No more."

He flicked the knife back and forth in front of Shea. Laughing, he turned to see Blade's reaction.

In one swift movement, the Dakota chieftain reached for a war lance displayed on the gallery wall. He leaned back, aimed, took two steps forward, and put all the skill and strength he'd displayed at the Ball into the throw.

Shea stared in disbelief as the lance streaked past her and pierced the bicep of Cheek's knife arm. The force of the throw pinned him to the stuffed buffalo like an insect on a display board.

An astonished grimace of pain contorted Cheek's fleshy face. Clawing at the lance, he screamed with a ferocity that chilled Shea to the bone. "Santeeee."

Blade raced to the canoe and stepped between them, wrenching the knife from the dealer's hand.

Screeching Blade's name over and over, Cheek grabbed the chieftain's arm with his free hand and head butted him in the chest.

The men clashed, grunting and cursing. They slipped into a more primitive time, a time when might, not right, won the battle. When survival mattered more than justice. When good did not always triumph over evil.

Knocked back into the canoe by the grappling men, Shea heard punches and moans but could see nothing. The acrid scent of sweat and anger and fear stung her nostrils. Tom-toms beat in the distance.

She had to get up. Help Blade.

She scrambled free as Blade ripped the coyote headdress from Cheek's head and pitched it aside. He broke loose from the dealer and made a slashing motion at him with the knife.

"No!" She screamed. But she was too late.

A thatch of long scraggly black hair sailed over their heads just as the gallery lights flashed on. The scalp landed at the feet of Lieutenant Jansen standing with his men in the gallery entrance.

Forty-One

More lights flashed on in the museum. Dragging a battered and bleeding Cullen Gerard, Blade's men rushed into the gallery behind Lieutenant Jansen.

Shea flew into Blade's arms before the lieutenant had a chance to arrest him for scalping Cheek. "No matter what happens," she whispered in his ear, "I'll stick by you. It was in the heat of the moment."

He hugged her a heartbeat longer, then held her at arms length. "What?"

"You were only protecting me," she insisted. "You didn't mean to scalp Cheek."

Blade erupted with laughter. "Look." He spun her around to face the dealer.

She squeezed her eyes closed, not wanting to see what was left of Cheek's bloody head.

"Look," Blade urged.

She opened first one eye, then the other. "What's going on?"

"That's what I'd like to know," Jansen said as he joined them. "Miss Scott's in a state of shock. Santee's men have Mr. Gerard trussed up like a prize pig." He pointed at Cheek, the lance still protruding from his arm. "And someone has shish kebabbed this character. Hey, Wolkalski, get a medic over here and get this guy loose."

The paramedics did a double-take when they saw Cheek pinned to the buffalo. A police photographer, snickering under his breath, took pictures of the crime scene before Wolkalski disengaged the dealer and cuffed him.

Jansen held up Cheek's scalp that had landed at his feet. "What's this?"

"It's a wig," Blade said. "Everything about Cheek is fake. He's no Indian, not even half."

"Not with that red hair," Four Bears said, joining them. He helped Ann along with a supporting arm.

Shea found it difficult to digest the information. She still reeled from believing Blade scalped the man.

They all stared at Cheek. With his black shoulder-length wig gone, Shea plainly saw that the artifact dealer harbored close-cropped red hair. The scalp above his orangey forehead glowed as pinkish-white as Cullen's.

"I knew there was something strange about his tan," she said. "He must have used 'sun tan in a bottle' to darken his skin."

"A cheap brand at that," Blade said. "Even the palms of his hands are orange from applying the dye."

Cheek snarled.

"But why?" Ann asked, regaining her composure.

"So we wouldn't know he and Cullen are brothers," Four Bears said, releasing Ann.

"What?" Shea and Ann said in unison.

Brothers? Shea glanced at Cullen, scuffed and tattered from his trip through the window, then at the snarling Cheek. Talk about screwed up DNA.

She looked back at Four Bears. He still wore his sober expression, but his eyes twinkled. For the first time since she'd met the stoic Indian, he looked as if he were enjoying himself.

"We found Gerard half-conscious out on the terrace." Four Bears rested his hand on the knife sheathed at his waist. "Before we brought him back into the museum, we persuaded him to tell the truth."

"You're right about them being brothers," Jansen said. "I wasn't buying anybody's story, so I checked all your backgrounds. Wait a minute." He motioned to Officer O'Reilly who was handcuffing Cullen. "Bring that buzzard over here." He turned back to the others. "Cullen and Cheek are half-brothers. Same redheaded mother but different fathers. Hence the different last names and builds but same red hair. They were street kids who didn't quite fit in. One skinny and passive and the other an overweight cry baby."

Cheek snarled again.

Shea frowned. "He obviously grew out of it."

"Cheek got in trouble early," Jansen continued. "Has a juvenile record. My guess is they developed a pattern of Cullen as the brains and Cheek the brawn and carried the collaboration over into their adult life."

"How did they come to know so much about artifacts?" Ann asked.

"They grew up in New York. Hid out in museums and art galleries to get away from bullies," Jansen answered, "acquiring knowledge by osmosis, I guess. And a taste for the better things in life. Once I started checking, so did the museums Gerard worked at. Seems their inventories don't match their records. Imagine that."

"What about Cullen's aristocratic accent?" Shea asked.

Jansen shrugged. "Took on sophisticated airs, I guess. Adopted the accent to distance himself from the New York streets and to impress the people he'd be soliciting for donations. With fake IDs and credentials, they devised a plan to steal artifacts from the museums that Cullen had been hired to salvage."

"So while Cullen appeared to be a lifesaver," Blade said, "raising money from generous patrons for a percentage of the take, he was really robbing the museums."

"And leaving fake artifacts in his wake, with no one the wiser," Shea guessed. "Until Ethan caught on."

This time Cullen snarled a few colorful words.

"I couldn't arrest them for Brumley's murder, though. Some facts were missing. Until now," Jansen admitted. "Maybe our friend Cheek can fill us in."

"Keep your mouth shut," Cullen warned his brother.

"That would be good for you, wouldn't it Mr. Gerard?" Jansen said. "You've got an alibi. You were in bed with Miss Scott."

Ann gasped, a pink flush creeping up her neck.

"Sorry, ma'am," Jansen apologized. He turned to Cheek. "That leaves you without an alibi the night Brumley died. Looks like you'll do hard time alone. Might even get the death penalty. Unless you cooperate."

Cheek's eyes grew wider at the mention of the death penalty. "It was his idea," he blurted, glaring at Cullen.

"Shut up, you toad," Cullen ordered.

"I'm not going down alone. I did three years for that job in Jersey while you got away scot-free. I'm not taking another rap for you."

"*Shut up.*"

"Don't you see, Cheek," Jansen taunted. "Your brother set up the alibi with Ann just in case you were caught. You'd be the only one without a defense."

Cheek glared at his brother. "Cullen was worried Brumley would go to the police while we was in Santa Fe. We flew back early and headed for the museum. It was late. We come in the back way so the guard wouldn't see us. Cullen got the alarm code from Ann's purse early on."

Ann visibly sagged. Shea supposed she was bidding goodbye to the Guggenheim.

"We found the old man in the hallway by the back door," Cheek continued.

"That would be Ethan Brumley?" Jansen clarified.

"Yeah, Brumley. He had the fake lance with him. Cullen tried to take it, saying he'd hold it for safe keeping. The old man refused. He started accusing us of things, getting too close to the truth."

"So, you decided to shut him up for good," Blade said, disdain evident in his tone.

Cheek nodded. "We heard someone coming. I clamped my hand over Brumley's mouth and dragged him outside. He broke loose just as Ann Scott came out the back door. He started to shout to her."

"And," Jansen prodded.

"So I stopped him." He shrugged as if he described swatting at a pesky fly. "I drilled him with the lance. He didn't die right away. Started staggering around. I was afraid he'd make it back to the door and Ann would see him. So I knocked him down and pushed the lance through him into the ground to hold him."

Shea winced at the graphic description of Ethan's death. She thought back to her escape through the forest. If Cheek had caught her… She stiffened at the memory. Blade drew her closer.

"Cullen intercepted Ann while I hid behind a tree. It was dark. She didn't see nothin'."

Ann pulled a tissue from a pants pocket and dabbed at her eyes.

"Cullen got Ann into bed to get the alarm code and to keep her quiet," he added as an extra twist of the knife. "He don't care nothin' for her."

"You jerk." Ann picked up the broken canoe paddle and slammed it into Cullen's chest.

Weakened from crashing through the window and being "interrogated" by Four Bears, he caved over. Wolkalski pulled him to his feet. "We need a medic," he said to the men finishing up with Cheek's arm.

"Now cut that out," Jansen scolded Ann.

"How did you know we were here?" Shea asked her friend.

Ann smoothed back her damp hair. "I'd just stepped out of the shower and was toweling off when I heard Cullen talking on the phone. I listened at the doorway and heard him say he'd meet the caller at the museum. By the time I dressed, he was gone. I was worried about him, so I grabbed my gun and came after him. I didn't think to check if it was loaded."

Four Bears pulled Ann's gun from his shirt and handed it to Jansen.

Jansen eyed Ann. "You got a permit for that?"

"Of course."

Reminded how Cullen had tricked her, Ann hit him with the canoe paddle again.

"O'Reilly, take that from her." Jansen dropped Ann's gun in an evidence bag. "We gotta have something left to prosecute. He already looks like he's been pushed through a plate glass window."

"Uh, that would be me," Shea said, and relayed her part of the story. "My gun is still under that glass showcase." She pointed to where the .38 had disappeared.

"I'll get it," Billy Quintella offered. Before Jansen could object, the young Indian scooted half-way under and brought out the gun.

Jansen cocked his head at Shea. "Got a permit for that?"

"On three continents," she responded.

He shook his head in disbelief but let it go. "What made you continue searching for an explanation for the forged lance? Cheek explained about the replicas in the kid's classroom."

"I just couldn't believe Blade wouldn't have remembered. Either he or one of his men made them."

She paused, then pulled a scrap of paper from her jean pocket and unfolded it. "I found this in Ethan's coat pocket." She handed it to Jansen.

"Both you women are packing heat. You withheld evidence. Miss McKenna, you broke into a museum—"

"The door was unlocked."

He sighed. "When did I lose control of this investigation?"

She ignored his sarcasm. "The note says, 'Blade is involved.' It doesn't say, 'Blade is guilty' or 'Blade is a forger.' As precise as Ethan was, he wouldn't have been vague concerning something he felt so strongly about. He had no difficulty voicing his opinion of Cullen and Cheek. I trusted his judgment. And Tom Bennett had said whoever made the fake lance was good—real good. You said yourself Lieutenant, one of the artisans had to be involved."

He nodded.

"Someone attacked Cullen," she continued. "Who I then mistakenly eliminated as a suspect. My bad. That left Cheek and one or more of the Indians." She glanced at her friend. "Ann told me Cullen had spent the night with her. So Cheek didn't have an alibi. My dilemma was in proving which of the artisans was his partner in crime."

She took her .38 from Billy and tucked it back in her waistband. "Billy, you're just too sweet to have gone against your chief and forged a relic or killed Ethan. Stick with the graphic T-shirts, honey." She pointed at the Spanish galleon sailing across his chest with the caption 'Go Home.' "They say a lot."

"And Elk Horn." She turned to the artisan. "You were so proud you'd been chosen to make the feathered dance bustles for the revitalized Dog Soldier Society. I couldn't believe you'd jeopardize that commission. I thought you tried to kill me tonight at the powwow," she said to Four Bears in a subdued voice.

The big Indian's brow pulled into a frown.

"He and Cheek are both dressed as Dog Soldiers," she explained to Jansen. "But now that I see them together, I can tell the difference. See," she pointed at Cheek's war paint, "the bottom half of his face is painted white and the top half black. Like the Indian I bumped into when I first arrived at the powwow, and like the one I blinded with my flash.

"Four Bears' face paint, however, is split vertical down the middle and forked on each side of his nose and mouth. The right half white. The left half black."

She smiled ruefully at Four Bears. "When someone's chasing you through the woods at night with a knife, you fail to notice little things like how a person's face is painted. I'm sorry I misjudged you."

He nodded his acceptance of her apology.

She peered into Blade's eyes. "And you, sir, were an enigma, running hot and cold. Constantly changing direction. Keeping your own council. But Ethan, Tom Bennett, and your men respected you, as did I. We couldn't all be wrong." She shrugged. "Besides, your tale was too convoluted not to be true. Why not just let Cheek kill me? He'd already threatened to do that in the storeroom, but you intervened." She grinned at him. "My hero."

Blade cast a self-effacing smile at her.

"Yeah, yeah," Jansen interrupted. "Find a tepee somewhere." He tugged on the bill of his baseball cap and addressed the roomful of people in a booming voice. "That pretty well wraps it up for now. Stick around while my men take your statements." He offered his hand to Blade. "My mistake. Sorry. I really thought you were as guilty as Cheek and Gerard."

Blade accepted his apology. "You'll understand if I don't ask you to become my blood brother? If Shea hadn't agreed to meet with Cullen to clear my name, I'd still be a suspect."

"That's true," the lieutenant admitted. "And so would you," he added, pointing to Four Bears. "And you. And you." He singled out each of Blade's men. "You were so loyal to your chief—until I checked into Cullen and Cheek's background, I thought you were *all* involved."

The paramedics strapped Cheek to a gurney, Wolkalski handcuffed him to the side bar, and they wheeled him out. The forensic team taped off the gallery entrance and began collecting evidence. Jansen personally escorted Cullen to a squad car while Wolkalski and other officers took statements. Finished with theirs, Shea and Blade strolled outside toward the Indian camp.

"I guess you found the note on my apartment door," she said, her mind still reeling from the night's events.

"I never made it back to your apartment," he said.

"Then how did you—?"

"I returned to the powwow to find Cheek, like we planned, but ran into Tom Bennett, instead. He said Cheek mentioned flying to Santa Fe, so my men and I headed for the airport."

Her hand brushed against his as they walked, and he took hold of it.

"We saw Cullen and Cheek driving toward the museum in Cullen's Bentley and followed. They went inside, leaving the door open. We thought it might be a trap, so we scouted around outside."

"I didn't see you."

"We circled the museum grounds. We must've been at the front entrance when you arrived in back. We saw Ann go in. And just as we passed one of the gallery windows, someone pitched Cullen through it. You."

He stopped walking and playfully felt her arm muscle.

"No big deal," she said. "I tackled him when he wasn't looking."

"It was still a brave act."

She felt herself blushing.

"I sent Billy to call Jansen and an ambulance," he said. "Elk Horn and Bear guarded Cullen while I slipped inside. You know the rest." He pulled her into his arms. "Why didn't you wait for me like we planned?"

"I was afraid we'd miss our chance to clear your name. I didn't know I was being set up."

"My ancestors were right. If you hadn't flushed out Cullen and Cheek, Jansen would still think I was in league with them. Your name will be sung around the council fires for many moons," he said in mock seriousness.

She laughed.

He kissed her forehead. "I'm not kidding. My people will want to thank you for your part in saving the clinic for them."

"That's not necessary. Besides," she said with resignation, "I'm scheduled next week to cover...something somewhere."

What was her assignment? She found it difficult to think with him standing so close. He still wore the loincloth and buckskin breeches and no shirt. As they strolled among the tepees, the glow from camp lanterns highlighted his taut chest. She remembered the smooth feel of his skin beneath her hands, and it sent ripples of pleasure through her.

"I'll be supervising the construction of the clinic on the reservation," he said.

The tom-toms stopped. Quiet settled around them.

"I suppose *National Geographic* or some other magazine

could use a photo spread on the Indians of South Dakota," she said. "But for now, I'm headed for—" Now where was it? Oh, yes. "Mexico. The temple ruins. In the jungle."

A wistful look filled Blade's eyes. Her heart ached. She knew what he was thinking. They may never see each other again.

She kissed him long and hard on the lips, then pulled away. "I'm glad I met you, Blade Santee." Her heart had stopped aching and was now breaking.

What's that country song? Got an achy-breaky heart.

"If I should want to contact you—in case *National Geographic* is interested?" she stammered.

He peered deeply into her eyes. "Call my studio in Santa Fe. Or at the reservation. The museum has both numbers." It was almost a plea.

"I'll do that."

He pulled her into his arms again. "I mean it, Shea. I won't be able to contact you in the jungles of Mexico. So you'll have to call me."

"I will. But for now, you have a clinic to build. And I have a Mayan temple calling my name."

He held her tighter. "But *we* still have tonight." he said and guided her toward a tepee.

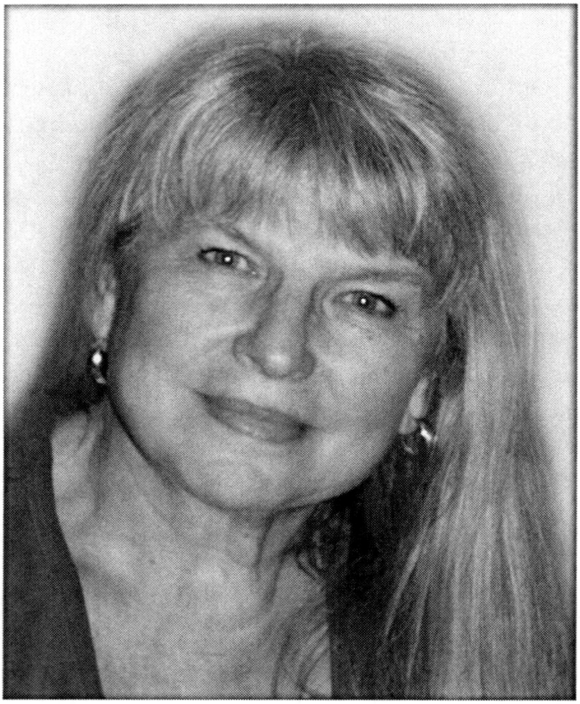

About Author Judy Moresi

Published articles, short stories, and photography to her credit, award winning author Judy Moresi is a member of Mystery Writers of America, Ozark Writers League, St. Louis Writers Guild, Missouri Writers Guild, and Sisters in Crime. She has spoken on mystery writing at the MWG 2010 Conference, the Killer Nashville Conference, and held a workshop at STLWG Writers in the Park. L&L Dreamspell launched her suspense novel, *Widow's Walk*, in 2010. Currently, she is hard at work on *Cat's Cradle*, the second book in her St. Mary's mystery series, and *Honky Tonk Man*, a female private eye mystery set in the world of Country Music.

Visit her website at www.JudyMoresi.com for event dates or contact her at tjmore232@charter.net

REVIEWS FOR WIDOW'S WALK

Judy Moresi's Widow's Walk features a unique setting, an engaging protagonist, and a plot full of surprises. The writing is tight and authoritative. With its gothic overtones, and plenty of comic relief, Moresi has a real winner on her hands. Save this one for a stormy night!

—Joanna Campbell Slan, Author of the Agatha-nominated *Paper, Scissors, Death*

I was prepared for a run-of-the-mill, first-time author effort. What I got was a pleasant surprise. Judy Moresi has scored big time with a suspenseful and well-crafted mystery that can hold its own with the most seasoned writer's work. The dialogue is crisp and believable, the characters are living, breathing individuals. Moresi doesn't hit a single false note in this incredible tale of murder and intrigue. One of the best books of its kind I've ever read.

—Esther Luttrell, Author and Screenwriter

The novel is set in an eerie complexity of who dunnits and whys obscured and dominated by an old decrepit Victorian mansion where murder in the past is whispered and talked about in conjecture with violence of the current. At any moment, with every page turned, the reader wonders who will die violently, who will survive.

—Two Mirrors "Times River," Atlanta, GA

Local author Judy Moresi's latest, Widow's Walk, may not sharpen your noggin but it sure is a page-turner. With shadowy figures creeping around an old house, a stalker and rumors that the main character's home is haunted, maybe you shouldn't hunker down with the tome at bedtime—unless you want to sleep with the bathroom light on.

—Sauce Magazine Review, St. Louis, MO

Laura [Chandler] has inherited a ramshackle Victorian manse complete with falling plaster, cobwebs, creaky stairs and its own ghost. It also comes with a menacing intruder, who writes chilling threats on her door and leaves an animal carcass in her kitchen… [Widow's Walk] gains appeal through the grit and determination of a plucky heroine who has a wry sense of humor.

—Shirley K. Murray, St. Louis Post-Dispatch Book Reviewer

Spooky read for a rainy night. A heroine inheriting a spooky, haunted house is one of my favorite premises and I have to say, Widow's Walk doesn't disappoint. Laura is smart, witty, creative, and disbelieving in the odd things happening around her, instead putting the blame on a resentful neighbor. There's even a love interest to quicken the heart of romantic readers. The villains are evil but not overdone and there's enough suspects roaming about to keep the reader guessing until the end. The twists and turns of Widow's Walk had me forgetting time, glued to the pages to find out what happened next. My only disappointment was that the book ended. Brava Ms. Moresi.

—P.S. Skochinski, Author in the high desert of California